THE BEAST UNDER THE WIZARD'S BRIDGE

JOHN BELLAIRS
By BRAD STRICKLAND

Piccadilly
PRESS

First published in Great Britain in 2020 by
Piccadilly Press
80-81 Wimpole St, London W1G 9RE
www.piccadillypress.co.uk

First published in the United States of America
by Dial Books for Young Readers, 2000

Text copyright © the Estate of John Bellairs, 2000
By Brad Strickland
Illustrations copyright © Nathan Collins, 2020

A CIP catalogue record for this book is available
from the British Library.

ISBN: 978-1-84812-872-9
Also available as an ebook

1 3 5 7 9 10 8 6 4 2

Typeset in Sabon LT Std by Palimpsest Book Production Ltd,
Falkirk, Stirlingshire

Printed and bound by Clays Ltd, Elcograf S.p.A.

Piccadilly Press is an imprint of Bonnier Books UK
www.bonnierbooks.co.uk

For Barbara,
with all my love.
B.S.

CHAPTER ONE

For many months Lewis Barnavelt had been worried. It all started when his uncle Jonathan looked up from the evening paper one snowy February afternoon. "Well," Uncle Jonathan had said softly, "the fools have done it. Progress is coming to Capharnaum County." He tossed the paper aside with a snort of disgust.

Lewis had been lying on his stomach in front of the Barnavelts' TV set, a nifty Zenith Stratosphere that had a round screen like a porthole. He pushed himself up from the prickly brown carpet and looked away from the cowboy movie to glance at Jonathan Barnavelt. "What's wrong?" asked Lewis.

His uncle, a heavyset, gentle man with red hair and a red beard streaked with white, shook his head. He put his thumbs in the pockets of his vest and frowned. "Oh, forget I said anything. Probably nothing." He wouldn't talk about it any more.

Later that evening Lewis looked through the paper for a clue as to what was bothering his uncle. He found an article on page three that might be it. The headline read COUNTY TO REPLACE BRIDGE. The story said that concerned citizens had complained about the old bridge over Wilder Creek. The county authorities had decided that the iron bridge was too narrow and in need of expensive repairs. Therefore, the county was going to replace the ageing structure with a modern concrete one. That bothered Lewis almost as much as it seemed to bother his uncle.

Lewis was a stocky kid with a round moon

face. He had been born in Wisconsin, and for the first ten years of his life he had lived in a town outside of Milwaukee. Then his mother and father both died in a terrible car crash, and Lewis had come to live with his uncle Jonathan in the town of New Zebedee, Michigan.

For a little while Lewis had been lonely and miserable. He was also a bit afraid of his uncle—but only at first. Soon he learned that Jonathan was a sorcerer whose magic was real. He could create wonderful three-dimensional illusions. And their neighbour Mrs Florence Zimmermann was an honest-to-goodness witch. A wrinkly faced, laughing, sprightly good witch who also happened to be a fabulous cook.

As time passed, Lewis grew to feel at home in New Zebedee. He and his best friend, Rose Rita Pottinger, were in junior high school. In many ways, Lewis remained timid and unsure of himself. Rose Rita called him a worrywart because his active imagination always pictured the very worst that could happen to him.

And yet, together with Rose Rita, Uncle

Jonathan, and Mrs Zimmermann, Lewis had shared some pretty frightening adventures. Still, he especially dreaded change of any kind. Maybe this was because of everything that had happened in his life after the death of his parents. Or maybe, as Uncle Jonathan had said one day, Lewis just naturally liked his life to remain comfortably the same from day to day.

Whatever the reason, any little alteration bothered Lewis. When Uncle Jonathan had all the wallpaper in their house at 100 High Street replaced, Lewis had been fidgety for weeks. Later, when Uncle Jonathan had given up smoking his stinky pipes on a dare from Mrs Zimmermann (who then had to give up her crooked little cigars), Lewis actually missed the odour.

And now the news that the county was going to replace the bridge over Wilder Creek depressed Lewis and made him jumpy. Of course, he had other reasons too.

He tried to explain these reasons to Rose Rita

about a month after he had read the newspaper story. Rose Rita was nearly a head taller than Lewis. She was a thin girl with long, straight brown hair and big black-rimmed glasses. She was also something of a tomboy, but Lewis admired her level-headed good sense. One day in March, on their way home from school, Lewis and Rose Rita stopped at Heemsoth's Rexall Drug Store to have a couple of sodas.

The soda counter was on the right side of the store as you entered, and it smelled wonderfully of hamburgers and coconut pie. Lewis and Rose Rita sat near the front, at a little round glass-topped table beside the window. Their chairs had frames of twisty wire painted white, with red leatherette cushions. Lewis liked them because when you sat on one, the air poofed out of it like an exasperated sigh, as if the chair were saying, "That's right, sit on me! Nobody cares about *my* feelings." At least, that's how he had felt when he was younger.

It was a bright, sunny day, but Lewis had been in a bad mood for weeks by then. Rose

Rita watched him as she slurped her soda. Finally, she said, "OK, Gloomy Guts. What's been on your mind lately? You're about as much fun as a toothache."

Lewis scowled and shook his head. "You wouldn't understand," he answered.

Rose Rita sat back in her chair and crossed her arms. "Try me. You might be surprised."

Lewis took a deep breath. "You know the old iron bridge out on Wilder Creek Road?" he asked. "Well, they're going to tear it down."

Rose Rita frowned. "So what? That's progress for you."

"Yeah," Lewis said glumly. "That's just what Uncle Jonathan said."

With a keen glance at his face, Rose Rita said, "This really bothers you. OK, Lewis, spill it."

Lewis stared at his half-finished soda. "You know a lot of it already. When I first came to New Zebedee, Mrs Zimmermann, Uncle Jonathan, and I had to face the ghost of Mrs Isaac Izard."

Rose Rita looked quickly around, but nobody

was near enough to overhear them. She leaned closer and said in a low voice, "You've told me about that. Old Isaac wanted to end the world, but he died before he could pull that off. Then his dead wife rose from the grave and tried to end the world with a super-duper magic clock the old wizard had hidden in the walls of your house."

"She nearly did it too," said Lewis. As he remembered the light gleaming off of Selenna Izard's glasses, he couldn't keep from shivering. "Well, what I've never told you is that one evening, Uncle Jonathan took Mrs Zimmermann and me out for a long drive. That was in November, and we were just riding around, seeing the sights. It was dark when we started back. Then Uncle Jonathan noticed the lights of a strange car coming up behind us."

Rose Rita listened in silence as Lewis told her the whole story. Uncle Jonathan had really been frightened, and Lewis had been practically terrified. When Lewis had been younger, he had often pretended that any car he was riding in was being followed by some car or other. That night, though, the game had been for real.

Lewis described how his uncle's car, an old Muggins Simoon, had sped through the darkness. On the motorway, Jonathan must have pushed the car to eighty or ninety miles per hour. The Muggins Simoon lurched dangerously around sharp curves, its tyres spitting stones and squealing as it crossed patches of gravel. Finally, Uncle Jonathan screeched the car into a tight turn at a place where three roads met. Lewis saw in one heartbeat a Civil War cannon white with frost, a wooden church with smeary stained-glass windows, and a general store with a dark, glimmering window that said SALADA. He could still close his eyes and see that scene in his imagination, like a picture in an album.

Then they were on Wilder Creek Road. With the mystery car hot on their trail, Mrs Zimmermann had hugged Lewis and spoken reassuring words. He still remembered how he had felt her heart beating fast with her own fear. That scared him even more than the frantic race.

At last Wilder Creek came in sight. Over it stood the iron bridge, a web of crisscrossing black girders. The old car had thundered across it, raising a rolling clatter from the bridge boards beneath the tyres. Sitting at the table with Rose Rita, Lewis gulped and broke off his story. He felt sick to his stomach just remembering that night. He pushed his soda away.

"What happened then?" asked Rose Rita in an urgent voice. "Lewis! Tell me!"

Taking in a deep, shaky breath, Lewis said, "Uncle Jonathan stopped the car and we got out. The ghost car had vanished."

"Because," said Rose Rita slowly and thoughtfully, "ghosts can't cross running water. I read that in *Dracula*."

"That's vampires," objected Lewis.

"Same difference," retorted Rose Rita. "A vampire's just a kind of blood-sucking ghost, you know."

"Well, anyway," said Lewis, "whatever it was,

it had disappeared. Mrs Zimmermann said it couldn't chase us any further partly because of the running water, but also because of something else. She meant the bridge."

Rose Rita made a rattling sound as she sipped the last of her soda through the straw. "What about the bridge?"

Lewis frowned. "It was made by—by somebody whose name I don't remember. But he put something special in the iron, Mrs Zimmermann said. It was supposed to keep the ghost of some dead relative from coming to get him."

Neither of them said anything for a minute. Then Rose Rita said softly, "This really bothers you. You've turned pale."

Lewis sighed sadly. "I know you think I worry too much about stuff like this, that I get all worked up over nothing. But just the thought of that bridge being torn down makes me—I don't know. I feel crawly inside, as if something bad is about to happen."

"Have you talked to your uncle about this?" asked Rose Rita.

With a grimace, Lewis shook his head. "The story in the newspaper bothered him a lot," he said. "I didn't want to pester him. I mean, he can't do anything about the bridge being torn down."

Rose Rita thought for a few seconds. "You finished with your soda?" Lewis nodded.

Rose Rita stood up. "Then let's go see Mrs Zimmermann about this. She'll know whether to worry, and what to do if there's really something to worry about. If the ghost of old what's-his-name's relative is going to come charging over the new concrete bridge, Mrs Zimmermann will deal with him."

Lewis smiled in a weak sort of way. Rose Rita liked Mrs Zimmermann immensely and trusted her judgement in everything—even though Lewis knew that Rose Rita's dad sometimes called Mrs Zimmermann "the town crackpot." And, come to that, Lewis had always found Florence Zimmermann a staunch friend. "OK," he said in a small voice. "But I hope she won't be upset."

They walked down Main Street, turned on to Mansion, and continued to High Street. Lewis and his uncle lived in a three-storey stone house at the top of a steep hill. A frilly wrought-iron fence crowned with pompon flowers ran around the yard, and an old chestnut tree shaded everything. When Lewis had first come to New Zebedee, he had thought the best part of his uncle's house was the turret, with a little oval window set in the shingles at the top, like a calmly watchful eye.

Right next to the Barnavelt house stood Mrs Zimmermann's. It was small but cosy, with a neatly trimmed yard and flower beds that, in the summer, were bright with petunias, asters, and nasturtiums. Often delicious aromas would drift over to the Barnavelts from their neighbour's house, and whenever they did, Mrs Zimmermann was sure to invite everyone over for a tasty meal or to show up at Jonathan's door with a plate of oatmeal-walnut cookies or a fudgy, gooey, delicious chocolate cake.

Today, Lewis couldn't smell anything cooking.

Rose Rita rang the doorbell, and Mrs Zimmermann opened the door a second later. She was a retired schoolteacher, and she looked as if she would have been a great one. Her wrinkly face easily broke into a wide smile, and her bright eyes could be mischievous and affectionate behind her gold-rimmed glasses. She loved purple, and she was wearing a purple flower-print housedress, with a purple scarf tied around her untidy mop of white hair. She grinned the moment she saw them. "Lewis and Rose Rita!" said Mrs Zimmermann. "What a pleasant surprise! Come on in. I'm just finishing some spring cleaning, and you can help me lug and tug my furniture back where it should be."

It didn't take long to do that, and then Mrs Zimmermann served them chocolate-chip cookies and milk at her kitchen table. "Now," she said briskly as she poured herself a cup of coffee. "You two have some deep, dark secret on your minds, or I'm not a witch. So what's troubling you, Lewis? Has old Frizzy Face conjured up some illusion he can't get rid of?"

Lewis had to smile at the thought. Sometimes Uncle Jonathan's illusions almost took on a life of their own, like the Fuse-Box Man who had once lived in the cellar, or Jailbird, the striped neighbourhood cat that still occasionally whistled tunes, though badly off-key. "No," he said. "Not this time."

"Lewis and his uncle are worried about the old bridge over Wilder Creek," said Rose Rita promptly. "We want to know if anything terrible will happen when it's torn down."

Mrs Zimmermann sat back in her chair, looking surprised. She touched her chin with her finger and murmured, "Good heavens, Rose Rita! You don't waste time getting to the point, do you?"

Even Mrs Zimmermann's yummy cookies didn't tempt Lewis. He moved his plate away and said, "Uncle Jonathan got upset when he read about the new bridge last month. And I know he's still worried, because he won't talk to me about it."

"Lewis told me that some wizard put a

magical spell on the bridge," said Rose Rita. "I knew you could give us the whole story."

Mrs Zimmermann chuckled. "'Come clean, or else,' is it? Well, my friends, there isn't really much that I can tell you. The iron bridge was constructed back in, oh, 1892. The man who built it was a rich fellow named Elihu Clabbernong. His family had been farmers for generations, and they used to own hundreds of acres between New Zebedee and Homer. People said that Elihu's old uncle Jebediah—I think Jebediah was really his granduncle—was a wicked magician. He had his own farm somewhere outside of town, and at night people passing by saw strange lights and heard eerie sounds. Well, when Elihu was just a young boy, both of his parents died mysteriously. Their will left everything to him, so their big farm was sold at auction and the money was put into a trust fund for Elihu. He came to live with his uncle."

Lewis felt goosebumps breaking out on his arms. "I don't like this story," he said in a quivering voice. "That's just what happened to me!"

Mrs Zimmermann leaned over and gave Lewis a friendly pat on the shoulder. "Except that *your* uncle is a very good man, Lewis. Even if he does play a lousy game of penny poker! Where was I? Elihu grew up on Jebediah's farm, and people say that his uncle taught him sorcery. I don't know anything about that. Elihu never talked about magic, and he never joined the Capharnaum County Magicians Society. The few times I saw him, he seemed perfectly normal—for a rich recluse, I mean."

"Do you mean he was some kind of hermit?" asked Rose Rita.

Mrs Zimmermann looked thoughtful. "You could say that. He pretty much minded his own business. At any rate, what I *do* know is that one December midnight in 1885, a meteor came whizzing through the skies. It lit up everything for miles around Capharnaum County. People said it was as red as blood, and that the weird light lingered behind it for ten minutes. The meteorite crashed to Earth somewhere past the barn on the Clabbernong farm with a tremendous explosion that made church bells ring and cracked windows all the way into town. That same night, just about the time the meteorite slammed down, old Jebediah died."

Lewis gulped. He asked, "Did the meteorite hit him?"

"Oh, no," replied Mrs Zimmermann. "I think the timing of his death was just a coincidence. Elihu was about twenty-two or twenty-three, so the farm and everything went straight to him. He had a mysterious bonfire the next day. People suppose that he burned Uncle Jebediah's evil magic books and papers. Then he burned his uncle."

"So he didn't really become a magician himself," said Rose Rita.

Mrs Zimmermann replied, "I don't think so. Maybe he considered himself too well-off to need magic. By then he could legally control the money that had been put in trust for him, and it had grown with interest over the years.

In the next weeks Elihu added to his wealth. He sold almost everything, abandoned the family farm, and moved into New Zebedee. Can you guess the one thing he didn't sell?"

Lewis shook his head.

Rose Rita bit her lip and screwed up her face as she thought hard. "The meteorite," she said at last.

"Bingo!" said Mrs Zimmermann. "Good guess, Rose Rita. I never saw the thing, but an older friend of mine did. She said it was not much bigger than a baseball, and that it gleamed with unearthly colours, colours she couldn't even describe. It made her nervous just to look at it, she told me, and it didn't do much for Elihu's nerves either. Even though Elihu had plenty of money, he was timid and jumpy and always acted as if something were following him. Finally, in 1892, seven years after his uncle's death, he offered to replace the old wooden bridge over Wilder Creek with an iron one. He would pay for the whole thing himself. Of course the county accepted. Now, they say that Elihu melted the meteorite down and mixed it into the iron used to make the bridge. At any rate, after the iron bridge was finished that autumn, Elihu was a happier man. He invested in banks and businesses. He got richer and richer, and he lived in New Zebedee right up until the time he died of natural causes. No ghost ever got him, so I suppose his bridge worked."

"So you're not worried?" asked Rose Rita.

With a sigh, Mrs Zimmermann shrugged. "The ghost of old Jebediah doesn't have anyone to come after. Elihu never married, and there are no other living Clabbernong descendants. So even if tearing the old bridge down lets that tormented spirit cross Wilder Creek, it has no victim it could haunt or hurt."

"Then why is my uncle so upset?" asked Lewis.

Giving him a kind smile, Mrs Zimmermann replied, "Well, Lewis, it could be that your uncle is more like you than you know. He doesn't care too much for change, and especially for any change that has to do with magic. Then too for many years now, I've realised that Jonathan Barnavelt, whatever he may say, is a first-class fretter!"

Rose Rita laughed at that. Even Lewis felt a little bit of relief.

But he was still concerned. And as more weeks went past, and March became April and April turned into May, his anxiety never went away, but just grew deeper. By the 1st June it was like an ache buried in his heart. An ache for which he could find no cure.

CHAPTER TWO

School ended for the summer, but even that didn't lighten Lewis's mood. On the last afternoon of the school year, Mrs Zimmermann announced that the next day she was going to give a picnic at her cottage on Lyon Lake, and everyone was invited. It would be the first Thursday of summer vacation. Lewis called Rose Rita, who was happy to come along. The water was still too cold for swimming, but they could play badminton, gorge on hamburgers, and relax.

Uncle Jonathan agreed to drive everyone in

his big old car. That Thursday morning was sunny and warm, with a clear blue sky. Still, Lewis wished he could shake the nagging sense of dread he felt. He had almost become used to it, but like a dull pain, it was something that he could never want to live with. He had finally convinced his uncle to stop buying him corduroy pants, and that morning he put on jeans, a pair of black trainers, and a white T-shirt.

Jonathan Barnavelt was dressed as usual in his tan khaki trousers, blue work shirt, red vest, and a ratty old tweed jacket. He lugged an enormous wicker picnic hamper over from Mrs Zimmermann's house and stored it in the boot. Mrs Zimmermann walked behind him, wearing a purple dress and a broad-brimmed purple sun hat. "Well, Lewis," she said as he opened the car door for her, "how does it feel to have the shackles off for the summer?"

"All right, I guess," said Lewis with a shy smile. He got into the back seat, Uncle Jonathan climbed in behind the steering wheel, and they were off in a cloud of exhaust smoke. They stopped at Rose Rita's house on Mansion Street just long enough to pick her up, and she came running out wearing trainers, jeans, and a baggy red T-shirt about two sizes too large for her.

She got in next to Lewis, and when Mrs Zimmermann repeated her question, Rose Rita grinned and said, "It feels great to be out of school! For one thing, I was getting sick up to here with plaid skirts and blue blouses!"

It was a pleasant morning, and Jonathan drove down Homer Road in a cheerful, relaxed mood. Mrs Zimmermann talked about what she was doing with her yard that year. She had planted some new kinds of flowers, daylilies and Shasta daisies and a bed of violets for which she had high hopes. "Violets are violet, after all," she said, "and that isn't too far from purple. And if they don't turn out purple enough, I'll just zap them with a little spell! What about you, Jonathan? Have you done anything special with your yard?"

"Well, Florence, I've been considering that very question. I'm thinking about paving it over with concrete," Jonathan said in a serious voice. "Then I could paint it green, and if I wanted flowers, I could buy some plastic ones, drill some holes in the concrete, and—"

"Oh, stop your teasing, Brush Mush," Mrs Zimmermann retorted.

They arrived at Mrs Zimmermann's cottage. While Uncle Jonathan and Mrs Zimmermann unloaded the hamper and got the grill ready, Lewis and Rose Rita put up the badminton net. They whacked the shuttlecock back and forth for a while, not really keeping score. Lewis was pretty good. He was more interested in keeping the game going as long as possible than in scoring points, so he almost always lobbed the shuttlecock. Sometimes Rose Rita was able to smash it past him, but they often managed to keep it flying between them for five or ten minutes at a stretch.

When Lewis and Rose Rita got tired of that, they switched to a game of horseshoes. Rose Rita was better at it than Lewis. With the pink tip of her tongue poking out of the corner of her mouth, she would take careful, deadly aim at the metal stake. Then she would toss her horseshoe spinning through the air, and as often as not, it would land around the stake with a loud clank! Lewis's horseshoes fell short or sometimes wound up leaning against the stake. "You going to Boy Scout Camp this summer?" Rose Rita asked Lewis.

Lewis shrugged as he picked up his next horseshoe. "I don't know. Uncle Jonathan and I haven't talked about it."

Rose Rita threw a shoe, which hit the stake and twirled around it noisily before thunking to earth. "Perfect!" she crowed. "Well, we're not going on a long vacation this year. Mum and Dad want to go to the Upper Peninsula for a week. Guess the rest of the time we'll just stick around New Zebedee."

Lewis pitched his horseshoe and missed the stake by a mile. "Uncle Jonathan hasn't mentioned vacations either. I think he wants to stay in town just in case."

"Just in case of what?" asked Rose Rita, sounding surprised.

Lewis gave her a quick look. He glanced over his shoulder. Near the cottage, Uncle Jonathan and Mrs Zimmermann were cooking at the grill, standing in a fragrant billow of hickory smoke. They were paying no attention to Lewis and Rose Rita. Still, Lewis lowered his voice to a whisper. "You know. They've opened the new bridge over Wilder Creek. I think the county's already tearing the old one down."

For a second Rose Rita looked at him as if he'd just announced he was visiting from the planet Mars and planned to marry the queen of England. Then understanding dawned in her eyes. "The old iron bridge?" she asked in a disbelieving voice. "Good grief, are you still fretting about that?"

Lewis shrugged dejectedly. "I can't get it off my mind."

Rose Rita blinked at him through her round glasses. "Lewis, why didn't you *say* something?"

"I didn't want to bother anybody," mumbled Lewis. "Look, there's nothing we can do if the county wants to tear down some stupid old bridge. Uncle Jonathan hasn't said anything about the bridge since last February, and when we asked Mrs Zimmermann, she didn't think there was anything to be afraid of. So I already know it's dumb of me, but—" He broke off, unable to finish the thought.

"But you can't help it," said Rose Rita sympathetically. "Hmm. Let me think about this. Maybe we can find some way to check up on things. If nothing else, we can make sure there's really nothing to worry about."

And there they left it for a time. Soon Uncle Jonathan called them to lunch, and they had a wonderful picnic meal on the grass near the lake. Mrs Zimmermann had a secret recipe for hamburgers that made them juicy and delicious, and she served creamy potato salad and some of her own dill pickles too. They weren't like the kind of flabby, squishy pickles that Jonathan bought at the supermarket but were crunchy and sour and salty all at once. For the first time in ages, Lewis ate with a good appetite.

Afterwards, they all pitched in to clean up,

and everyone lazed around in the afternoon. Uncle Jonathan produced a deck of cards, and for a couple of hours, they sat outside around a folding card table playing silly penny poker games. Jonathan lost most of the time, grumbling in a good-natured way that he preferred straight five-card draw. "The trouble with these games," he said, "is that I can't even remember the crazy rules!"

"Very well," said Mrs Zimmermann, who had the next turn to deal. "We'll play something simple. Now, in this game, jacks, sevens, and red threes are wild—"

Jonathan groaned, but he was laughing at the same time.

It was a good way to pass a warm, drowsy afternoon. Finally, towards four o'clock, everyone was ready to head back to New Zebedee.

"Why don't we all go to a movie tonight?" asked Mrs Zimmermann as they took the folding chairs and table back into her cottage. "I think there's a pirate film showing downtown. If it's a good one, Jonathan can re-create all the battles with one of his spells, and we'll take turns being the pirate captain." They came outside again and Mrs Zimmermann locked the door.

Lewis thought the movie sounded like fun, but before he could say anything, Rose Rita asked, "On the way back to town could we go see the new bridge over Wilder Creek?"

Mrs Zimmermann looked at her sharply, and Uncle Jonathan, who was putting the hamper in the boot of his big old car, froze. He turned slowly around. "That's a strange idea, Rose Rita! What put it into your head?"

With an innocent smile, Rose Rita said, "I just wondered what the new bridge is like, that's all. And if they're taking down the old one."

Uncle Jonathan exchanged a look with Mrs Zimmermann. To Lewis it seemed to be a dark look, as if Uncle Jonathan were asking a question without speaking aloud. Mrs Zimmermann gave him a quick, short nod, really just a downwards jerk of her chin.

"Sure, why not?" Uncle Jonathan asked in a

hearty voice. "We can take Twelve Mile Road over to Wilder Creek Road. I haven't been out that way lately myself. We might as well see how the construction is going."

Lewis opened the door for Rose Rita, and as she started to get in the car, he whispered, "What's the big idea?"

"Just checking up," Rose Rita whispered back. "We'll watch your uncle and Mrs Zimmermann. If something is wrong, those two will know it!"

Lewis swallowed hard, but he climbed into the back seat beside Rose Rita. Maybe it would be better to know than to remain in an agony of uncertainty. They left the cottage, and after a while, Jonathan took a little back road. It wasn't even paved, just covered with loose gravel that crunched and popped under the old car's big balloon tyres. Mrs Zimmermann said, "I thought we were heading for Twelve Mile Road."

"Shortcut," said Uncle Jonathan with a grunt. For some minutes the car moved over the gravel, travelling slowly. Looking out his window, Lewis saw some pretty wild land, overgrown pastures, woods that seemed to have run riot with thick growths of thorny brush, and here and there, an abandoned farmhouse or two. Jonathan slowed the car to a crawl.

"Looks like there's been a forest fire," said Rose Rita.

Lewis felt his heart thud. Off to the right, a big patch of ground, several acres at least, was dead. The trees were leafless, the bark crumbling off their trunks. Their branches and twigs seemed to claw up at the sky in desperation, as if the trees had tried frantically to escape before they died. The stubble on the ground lay grey and lifeless. A farmhouse near the centre of this desolate land didn't look burned, but it was ruined. Its rusty red tin roof had fallen in, and the windows gaped dark and empty, like the eye sockets of a skull. Lewis wrinkled his nose. The place had a sickening smell, faintly sweet but rotten too, with a strong, bitter tinge of mildew. He knew with every ounce of his being that some evil thing had visited this patch of barren earth.

"Jonathan," said Mrs Zimmermann in a testy voice, "I think we could safely go a little faster than this."

Jonathan put his foot on the accelerator, and the car rolled away from the blasted farm. The trees began to have leaves again, and soon everything looked normal. Deserted, but normal. Then the gravel road led on to Twelve Mile Road, which was paved with asphalt. They turned, and before very long they reached the spot that Lewis still saw sometimes in his nightmares. A rusty Civil War cannon stood in a grassy triangular park. An old white country church with dusty stained-glass windows was on one side of the road, and across from it stood a general store with a green SALADA sign in its window. This was where Jonathan had made a desperate screeching turn that night when Lewis was only ten and the ghost of Mrs Izard had been pursuing them in a deadly race.

The car was on Wilder Creek Road now,

heading towards New Zebedee. No one said anything as the road wound its way over hills and past farms. At last they came to the top of a high hill, and below them Lewis could see Wilder Creek winding in the afternoon sunlight. To the left, the old iron bridge still spanned the water. The road had been closed off for several hundred yards on either side of it. To replace that stretch, a new part of the road had been created, and its black asphalt gleamed. Straight ahead, a modern concrete bridge took the road right across the creek. The time was past five o'clock, and the workmen had finished for the day, but their equipment still stood around, yellow bulldozers, cranes, and other construction machinery. Jonathan slowly drove across the concrete bridge, then found a place to pull off the road and park.

They all climbed out and walked back along the shoulder of the road. Lewis could see that the workmen had already removed the wooden bridge boards from the black iron framework of the old span. Some of the girders had been taken down and lay in a careless pile off to the side. Everyone walked right up to the edge of the old bridge. Looking down where the boards used to be, Lewis could see the creek flowing smoothly underneath. It wasn't much of a drop to the water's surface, not much more than ten feet, but Lewis felt woozy and dizzy, as if he were looking over a high cliff. The world seemed to spin around his head. He backed away and stepped on something hard.

Lewis moved his foot and found that he had stepped on a loose iron rivet, about three inches long. It must have fallen out of one of the girders when the workmen were taking the old bridge apart. Without really thinking, he reached down and picked it up. The rivet felt strangely heavy in his hand, solid and warm. And the warmth was not like that of iron left in the sun, not exactly. Somehow—Lewis could not have said how—the piece of metal felt almost alive, as if it produced its own heat. Lewis turned the rivet this way and that, looking at it in the fading sunlight. Its surface glistened, untouched by rust.

Lewis could hardly believe that the rivet had been in the bridge for many years. It showed no corrosion. It might have been forged just that morning.

Lewis shook his head. Rose Rita had said something to him. Hurriedly, he dropped the rivet into his front jeans pocket, where it felt heavy but comforting. "Huh?" he said.

Rose Rita hadn't been looking at Lewis, but at the two adults, who stood about fifteen feet away. She glanced at him, pushing her glasses back into place on her nose. "I said, nothing seems too horrible."

"Oh," said Lewis. "No, I guess not."

Uncle Jonathan and Mrs Zimmermann had their heads together, carrying on a soft conversation that Lewis could not hear. Finally, Uncle Jonathan nodded.

He turned towards them and declared, "Kids, I guess I deserve the prize for being the world's biggest worrier, but Frizzy Wig tells me she can't sense anything wrong here. And if Florence can't find it, it isn't there. Lewis, I'm sorry that

I upset you back when we first heard the news about this old bridge. Anyway, it appears that all my anxiety was wasted. We'll keep an eye out, just in case, but I'll take Pruny's word any day, and she says there doesn't seem to be anything to be concerned about."

That might have ended it. They drove back to New Zebedee, saw their movie, and dropped Rose Rita off at her house. By the time Lewis went to bed, it was nearly ten, and he was tired. He took the rivet out of his jeans pocket and put it on the table beside his bed, next to his alarm clock and reading lamp. Then he switched off the light and hopped between the sheets.

For a few minutes he lay there in the dark, with his eyes closed. In his imagination he was aboard the pirate ship in the movie, climbing the shrouds to the maintop, fighting a ferocious cutlass duel along the yardarm, then getting to the deck by thrusting his sword into the mainsail, jumping, and holding on to the sword hilt as the blade ripped its way down the sail. Lewis could almost hear the clang of steel and the explosions of the cannon. He could all but smell the firecracker scent of smoke.

An enormous yawn interrupted his train of thought. He opened his eyes and looked over towards the luminous hands of the clock to see what time it was. Then, with a gasp, he sat up in bed.

The rivet was glowing in the dark. Colours crawled along its iron surface, writhing and shimmering like the rainbow hues you see if a drop of oil is spilled on to wet concrete. Lewis had learned a funny-sounding name to remember all the colours of the rainbow: Roy G. Biv. That stood for "Red, orange, yellow, green, blue, indigo, and violet." All those tints were there.

But he also saw colours that he could not identify. Colours that seemed to come from some place other than this world.

And all of them glowed softly in the darkness beside his bed.

CHAPTER THREE

That Saturday night Lewis had the first of many bad dreams. In this one, he, Mrs Zimmermann, Rose Rita, and Uncle Jonathan were at some zoo. It was unlike any real place Lewis had ever seen. All the animal cages were vast, tall structures of black iron bars, so heavy that sometimes it was hard to see the restless animals pacing back and forth behind them.

In the dream Lewis had the creepy feeling of déjà vu, the sense that all this had happened to him before and that he knew what was going to happen next. As they all walked slowly between one enormous cage containing a herd of shuffling elephants and another that held a dozen tall, brown-spotted giraffes, Lewis *knew* that Mrs Zimmermann was about to say, "I wish we could see more of the animals and less of the cages." An oppressive feeling came over Lewis. If Mrs Zimmermann said that, something terrible was going to happen. Lewis turned to ask Mrs Zimmermann not to speak.

Too late. Pulling her purple shawl more tightly around her shoulders, Mrs Zimmermann said, "I wish we could see more of the animals and less of the cages."

The words echoed in Lewis's brain. Somehow he knew a gruesome fate awaited them all. From every cage came loud trumpetings, snarls, roars, and screeches.

Everything about this place is wrong, Lewis thought desperately. Without his understanding how it happened, they were riding on a miniature train. A black locomotive chuffed and huffed, and the cars clattered along a narrow track. Lewis and Rose Rita rode in the car just behind the locomotive, and behind them were Uncle Jonathan and Mrs Zimmermann. A round iron safety bar swung down over their knees to hold them in place. The engineer was a tall, spindly man, all knees and elbows. He wore overalls, but instead of a blue-striped engineer's cap, he had a shiny top hat so deeply black that the reflections in its silk were midnight blue. The driver blew the train whistle with great enthusiasm, but the sound was anything but cheerful. Its low, mournful *whoo-ooo-ooo-ooo*! made Lewis think of dark nights, lonely graveyards, and staring owls. Ahead of them was the dark opening of a tunnel.

"I'm afraid of tunnels," said Rose Rita.

Lewis remembered that Rose Rita had a bad case of claustrophobia. Any closed-in space soon gave her the heebie-jeebies, and if the space was small, she would quickly get terrified and be unable to breathe.

The train dove into the dark arch. They plunged down a steep incline so fast that Lewis could not even catch his breath. He heard Rose Rita shriek, a thin, panic-stricken scream. Wind whistled past his face. He felt as if the train had run off the edge of the world and was falling through space, falling forever.

Lewis closed his eyes, clenching the iron safety bar. He heard a *whoosh*! and opened his eyes. The train had shot out of the tunnel. Now the tracks ran right between two rows of drooping willow trees that dripped their branches so low, the leaves brushed their hair. Though Lewis still had the impression of tremendous speed, the cars seemed to be moving slowly, no more than five or ten miles an hour. Lewis looked sideways at Rose Rita and was not surprised to see her face had turned a sickly green with fright. He knew, he *knew*, that she was going to ask him if it was over.

She looked at him. "Lewis, is it over?"

"I don't think so," replied Lewis forlornly. Like green curtains being pulled aside in a theatre, the willows parted. Ahead of the locomotive loomed the biggest cage yet, an iron monstrosity that towered up to the clouds, taller than any

skyscraper. Something slow moved behind the black bars. Something obscure, something huge. The train slowed to a crawl and then stopped. Lewis saw the track ended in the grass, as if it had been cut off, or never completed.

Suddenly the engineer leaped out and turned. Lewis heard the shocked gasps of his uncle and Mrs Zimmermann. Rose Rita cried out in alarm.

The engineer was a skeleton. His face was a grinning skull. He made an elaborate bow and swept the top hat off the ivory dome of his head. "End of the line!" he screamed in a horrible high-pitched voice. "End of the line and feeding time!"

He vanished. Lewis and Rose Rita struggled to get out of the train, but the bars across their laps held them in a tight and deadly grip. The cage before them began to sway, its metal bars creaking and groaning. The dark, shapeless mass it held stared at them with a yellow eye. It made a nasty, snuffling, grunting sound, like a hungry hog. Something smooth and slimy, resembling the tentacle of an octopus, wrapped around one of the bars and shook it.

Like a house of cards, the cage fell apart. Iron girders fifty feet long and a foot in diameter came tumbling down. They blocked out the sun. Lewis looked up and saw them falling on top of him, ready to crush the life from him—

With a dry scream, Lewis sat up in bed. He choked for air. For a minute he didn't know where he was or how he got there. Then he realised he was safe in his own room, that it had all been a nightmare. He looked fearfully at his bedside table, but the rivet was no longer glowing with those unearthly colours. Instead, he saw the familiar greenish-yellow hands of his alarm clock: 4:24.

For a little while Lewis lay still, letting his heart return to its normal beat. His throat and mouth were parched, as if he had been travelling in a desert. He had to get a drink of water.

Lewis switched on his lamp and slipped out of bed. He walked barefoot to the bathroom, but the paper-cup dispenser was empty. He would have to go downstairs.

Normally, that wouldn't have bothered him.

Uncle Jonathan's mansion was eccentric, with a few magical touches here and there, but Lewis knew it held nothing that could hurt him. He gathered his courage and went down the back stairway, the one with the odd oval stained-glass window. Jonathan had tried out a magic spell on it long ago, and the spell had never worn off. The window changed from time to time. When Lewis had first come to live with Jonathan, it had pictured a red-tomato sun setting in a sea the colour of old medicine bottles. During the next few years, it had shown many different scenes. Lewis glanced at it as he reached the landing, and then he froze, puzzled. The window was red, a lurid scarlet that glowed with its own light. Across it, in yellow capital letters, was the single word CAVE as if advertising the famous Carlsbad Caverns or Mammoth Cave.

Lewis didn't know of any caves anywhere close to New Zebedee. Maybe the magic had gone a little cuckoo, he thought. He headed for the kitchen, but the soft sound of voices stopped him. Mrs Zimmermann and his uncle were sitting in the study talking quietly. What could have brought Mrs Zimmermann over at that hour of the morning?

Walking on tiptoe, Lewis paused just beside the study door. It was ajar, and through the inch-wide opening he could clearly hear Mrs Zimmermann's tired voice: "Very well, Jonathan. We'll keep an eye on that bridge. Mind you, I think that whatever spook was after old Elihu has long since gone to its reward. I didn't feel anything when we were at the bridge, and I've checked my crystal ball since then. Nothing. But I know you too well to make fun of you if the old bridge has really given you the screaming meemies."

Lewis heard his uncle take in a long, slow, deep breath. "It isn't that exactly, Florence. Oh, I don't know—maybe it all has to do with the Izards. I spent ten years or so helping fight the evil those two nasty buzzards stirred up. The night that old Creepy Drawers almost caught us on Wilder Creek Road was one of the worst evenings of my life. Still, I have a bad case of what Shakespeare might call itchy thumbs. You remember *Macbeth*?"

Making her voice cackly and creepy, Mrs Zimmermann recited, "'By the pricking of my thumbs, something wicked this way comes'!"

"Exactly," responded Jonathan. "Exactly. And of course you know why I took my little detour on the way to the bridge."

"You bet your boots I do," answered Mrs Zimmermann tartly. "To check on the old Jebediah Clabbernong farm. Well, it's still as dead as ever. If I might say so, Jonathan, that was *not* one of your brighter ideas! I wouldn't have minded checking out the place with you, but to bring Lewis and Rose Rita along—well, I'm glad nothing happened."

For several seconds Jonathan did not answer. Then Lewis heard him say, "Florence, did you ever walk around on that farm? Did you ever touch one of the dead trees?"

"Ugh!" replied Mrs Zimmermann, and Lewis could picture her shuddering elaborately. "No, thank you! I'd just as soon plunge my hand into a bucket of squirming slimy slugs!"

"Well, I've tried it," Jonathan said. "And between you and me, I'd also prefer the slugs. Anyway, many years ago, I went exploring there one day. When you walk across that dead grass, it crunches to gritty powder under your feet. And when you put your hand against one of those tree trunks and push, your hand just sinks inside. The stuff doesn't feel like wood. It's more like sticking your hand into a crumbly old hornets' nest—"

"Empty, I hope," put in Mrs Zimmermann.

Jonathan chuckled without much humour. "Well, *I* didn't get stung at least. But I'm not kidding. You could drive your hand through one of those trunks if you wanted. Isn't it odd that after all these years, none of them has fallen? You'd think that the first good storm would blast them to smithereens."

"I wouldn't think about it at all, given the choice," replied Mrs Zimmermann. "So what happened?"

"A little after that, I got scared," admitted Uncle Jonathan. "I got scared, and I hurried away from there, and I've never set foot in the place again. Florence, it's uncanny. It's as if the very life of everything on that farm was—was sucked right out of it!" He dropped his voice. "I didn't tell you the worst thing I saw."

Lewis heard Mrs Zimmermann take a deep breath that time. "All right," she said in a steady voice. "What was the worst?"

"I think it was a woodchuck," answered Jonathan, his voice shaky. "It was that size, anyway. Some burrowing animal the size of a small dog. It was halfway out of its hole. It had no fur left. Its skin was that wrinkled, greyish-white colour of a dried wasps' nest. If I had to guess, I'd say it had been halfway out of that burrow ever since the night in 1885 when the meteor crashed to Earth just behind the old farmhouse."

"And it was just like the trees, I suppose," said Mrs Zimmermann. "That *is* pretty bad."

"It's worse than that," muttered Uncle Jonathan

in a voice so soft, Lewis had to put his ear almost up to the crack in the door to hear him. In fact, Lewis was so close that he could smell the aroma of coffee. His uncle was saying, "I didn't want to touch that—that *thing*, not after the way the tree had felt. I walked a couple of hundred feet off the farm, found a fallen branch that was pretty solid, and walked back. I pushed the stick into the creature's back. It sank right in with an awful crackling sound."

"Ugh," cried Mrs Zimmermann. "I don't think I can finish this cup now. Just as well. That picture's going to keep me up the rest of the night, anyway."

"Florence," whispered Uncle Jonathan. "Florence—it—*it moved*."

Lewis had to brace himself against the wall with one hand. He felt his stomach lurch. The coffee smell was suddenly very strong, so strong that it sickened him.

"Oh, Jonathan," said Mrs Zimmermann, her voice appalled. "You never said anything."

"The memory of it has haunted my nightmares

ever since," said Jonathan. "I didn't want to burden you too. Not until now. Now I think I have to. Florence, the poor creature tried to creep out of its burrow. It made a ghastly hissing sound—trying to breathe, I think. Both of its front paws snapped off the second it tried to drag itself forwards. Its body was splitting open. I—I pulverised it. I used that branch to pound it to powder." Lewis heard his uncle gasp. Then he continued, "I put it out of its misery. At least, I hope I did. To think otherwise—to think that the nasty pile of gritty powder I left behind still had some kind of unholy life in it—that's too much for me."

Lewis heard the hiss of breath, and he realised that Mrs Zimmermann had just exhaled. "That's more than enough for me too," she said in a low voice. "Very well. We'll mobilise the Capharnaum County Magicians Society. We'll all keep a weather eye out, an ear to the ground, and our noses to the grindstone. And then while we're in that ridiculous posture, someone will probably sneak up behind us and give us a good swift kick in the seat of the pants!"

Lewis heard his uncle give a weak little laugh. "I think we'd better watch you-know-who, as well. I haven't trusted those two since this whole bridge business began. If anybody is going to get involved in some kind of diabolical mischief around here, it will be that pair, you mark my words."

Lewis felt crushed. Was his uncle talking about Rose Rita and him? When he thought about it, he feared it might be so. In Lewis's mind, memories of all the times in the past when he had disobeyed his uncle rose up. He remembered occasions when his thoughtlessness had put them all in danger. His heart sank. He crept back upstairs feeling as lonely as he had ever felt in his life. He stopped in the bathroom and drank by ducking his head sideways in the sink and sucking in a trickle of water. Then he dragged himself back to bed.

What if his uncle had really lost all trust in

Lewis? What if he decided to send him away? Lewis knew one boy who had become such a problem that his parents had shipped him off to a military school. What if that happened to him? How could he even live without Rose Rita's friendship or Mrs Zimmermann's kindness and concern or his uncle's unfailing good humour?

Hunched beneath the thin sheet, Lewis felt alone and abandoned. And then he had another thought, a very disturbing one.

CAVE, the stained-glass window had said. That was an English word, but English was not the only language in the world. Lewis had also studied Latin at school. As it happened, *cave* was a perfectly good Latin word, but it had nothing to do with caverns or stalactites or stalagmites.

Instead, in Latin the word was a warning.

It meant—

BEWARE!

CHAPTER FOUR

Lewis had no way of knowing it, but at the same time as he was eavesdropping on his uncle and Mrs Zimmermann, another couple was having a heated conversation outside of New Zebedee. Like Uncle Jonathan, the woman had pulled her car off on the side of Wilder Creek Road not far from the skeletal old bridge. Then she had climbed out of the car, a battered black Buick. For a few moments she looked up and down the asphalt road, but at that hour of the morning, no traffic moved on it and no light showed, not even from a distant farmhouse. The eastern horizon lay still and dark, with no sign yet of dawn.

Everything was quiet, except for the faint, distant howling of a farm dog far away. A yellow rind of moon sailed low in the sky. It gave off a little light, just enough to see the outlines of things. Weak moonlight gleamed dully on the old car's wheels and bonnet.

The woman went around to the passenger side to help a shaky old man climb out. They both appeared to be about the same age, nearly eighty, but she was tall, with a tight bun of glimmering white hair, and she moved with a spring in her step. Despite the warm night, she wore a long dark coat that came to her ankles and was buttoned up to her chin. The man she assisted was slow, bald, bent, and quarrelsome. He was wearing a black suit over a white shirt, its collar open. He struggled from the car. "I can get out on my own," he growled, slapping at the woman's hands. "You go open the boot!" He stood tottering on the grassy shoulder, shaking his egg like head from side to side and leaning with all his weight on a walking stick.

"Just don't fall and break your neck, you old fool," returned the woman in a sour, flat voice. "Not now. Not when the time is so close."

The old man straightened his back with a jerk and waved his walking stick at her. Leaning on the cane again, he limped to the rear of the car and watched as the woman unlocked the boot and took out something long and tubular. In the dimness it looked like a five-foot length of cardboard tubing used to wrap carpets around. She carefully set this on end, then took out a heavy wooden tripod. "Where do you want me to set it up?" she asked.

The man gestured wildly with his cane. "Anywhere! Anywhere! We know the altitude and the azimuth, so it's all the same! Just find a good level spot. Hurry!"

With the folded tripod under one arm, the woman walked towards the old bridge. Though the workmen had changed the course of Wilder Creek Road, a short strip of asphalt leading on to the old bridge had not been torn up. She set the tripod on this. It snapped open with a clack, and she grunted as she tightened the legs. The tripod supported a heavy-looking mount of some kind.

When the woman finished with the tripod, she went back to get the tube. The old man walked beside her on the way to the car and back, grumbling and complaining the whole time. The woman refused to be hurried. Moving slowly but with assurance, as if she had done the same thing in the dark hundreds of times, she attached the tube to the mount. Twirling some round chrome knobs, she tilted the tube up towards the sky, and at last anyone could have seen it was a reflecting telescope, the kind that uses a mirror instead of a lens to magnify the image.

Humming a slow, gloomy tune, the woman fitted an eyepiece into its holder on the side of the tube. Then from her coat pocket she took a penlight with a red bulb. She switched it on. In the faint, ruddy glow, she adjusted first the tripod, then the telescope, studying a compass and two metal rings that were set into the mount. The rings were etched with lines and numbers, as if they were some kind of circular ruler. When the woman seemed satisfied with the numbers showing on each ring, she switched off the penlight and dropped it back into her pocket.

She pushed a button on the telescope mount, and a clockwork motor began ticking softly. "That should be right," she said. In a sarcastic, sneering tone, she added, "Should I check the view, or do you want to have the first look, O great lord and master?"

"Shut up, shut up!" snarled the old man, his voice trembling with anger. "I'll look! You wouldn't know it if you saw it!"

The woman sniffed, but she didn't reply. The man hobbled to the telescope, and being careful not to touch the tube, he peered into the eyepiece. Muttering, he twiddled a knob to focus the instrument. At once he broke into a delighted cackle. "I see it!" he announced. "I see it! Beautiful! Like a hairy little red star, and right smack in the centre of the field of view. Oh, well done, my darling wife! Just think, the last time it came towards Earth, the inhabitants of lost Atlantis cowered beneath its light! Fourteen thousand years have passed, and now the Red Star returns!"

"It's a comet, you old fool," returned the woman. "Well? Do I get a look?"

The old man stepped away from the telescope. "Certainly, my dear Ermine. Gaze upon it. Look your fill." As the woman bent over the eyepiece, the man stared up into the dark night sky. He said, "It is still invisible to the naked eye. But it is coming closer every moment. Soon, soon it will blaze in the sky! And our hour will come around at last!" The idea seemed to move him. He shook with a sob.

The woman did not look up from the eyepiece. The old man fished a crumpled handkerchief from his trouser pocket and limped towards the old bridge, wiping his eyes and blowing his nose. He stopped at the very edge of the bridge, staring down into a swirl of dark water. There was nothing to see but a rippling reflection of the faint moon. Suddenly the surface boiled

with a gurgling foam of bubbles, phosphorescent in the night. The old man laughed. "Soon, my pet, soon! Soon you will be free to do the bidding of Mephistopheles Moote! And a world full of fools will bow and cringe before me!"

The bubbles trailed away. A ghastly stench rose, a sick, faintly sweet scent of rotting flesh and mildew. But from the way the old man cackled and capered, it might as well have been the fragrance of roses.

The morning after his terrible dream, Lewis went to church with his uncle. St George's Church was a small stone building with oversized stained-glass windows That Sunday Lewis sat beside his uncle wondering if Jonathan really trusted him. The thought that maybe he didn't made Lewis despondent. As they left the church, Lewis paused to say a short prayer, and to light candles for the souls of his mother and father. Riding back home in the old Muggins Simoon, he resolved to prove himself worthy of being trusted.

The rest of the day passed normally enough. On Monday, Lewis told Rose Rita that he was afraid Uncle Jonathan was upset with them, but he didn't spell out exactly why. Lewis felt bad enough on his own. He didn't need to plunge Rose Rita into sorrow and uncertainty as well.

Rose Rita had heard enough, though, to want to help. "We could start," she suggested, "by finding out about this red meteor that whomped into old Clabberhead's farm back in 1885. In a quiet little town like New Zebedee, I'll bet something like that made the news. Come on."

Lewis followed her to the public library. They went down to the basement, where back issues of the town newspaper, the New Zebedee *Chronicle*, were stored. The papers had been bound into huge volumes with crumbling maroon covers and gilt numbers that had faded and flaked so much, they were hard to read. Some volumes were missing altogether, especially ones from the Civil War years, 1861 to 1865. Both of the volumes for the year 1885 were on the shelf, however, and Lewis and Rose Rita pulled down the second one, which ran from July to December.

"Mrs Zimmermann said the meteor hit in December," said Rose Rita, carefully turning the yellowed, brittle pages of the old newspapers. A thin dust rose, tingling in Lewis's nostrils and smelling faintly like sage.

Lewis saw the old papers had no photographs at all, just occasional engravings. Many of these were for ads selling such things as New, Improved Cultivators or kerosene stoves. Rose Rita got to the papers for December, and they began to scan through each one, looking for news of the meteor.

They found it at last in the paper for Tuesday 22nd December, in a story on page one. Lewis and Rose Rita leaned over the paper, their heads close together, and read:

ASTONISHING VISITOR FROM
THE STARS!

The goddess Diana, whose sphere is the moon, must have felt properly outraged at midnight last night. A shooting star from the depths of unknown space hurtled across the heavens, dimming her lustre and no doubt sending the maiden goddess to sulk in her boudoir.

Residents of New Zebedee, Eldridge Corners, Homer, and surrounding hamlets in Capharnaum County were rudely awakened at precisely midnight by a rushing, roaring sound, as of a gigantic skyrocket.

Constable James Andrews of New Zebedee, whose watchful eye was alert at the time, reported that the culprit was a meteor "as big as a house." It arched through the cold, clear, midnight skies with a deafening rumble, and it shed a brilliant crimson glare, so bright that "everything looked like it had been splashed with blood," said the good Constable.

The uproar was so loud that some sprang from their beds and fell to unaccustomed prayer, persuaded that the Last Trump had sounded and the end of the world was at hand. The vibrations caused by the meteor's passage shook all the church steeples in New Zebedee, thereby causing the bells to clang. About two score indignant citizens have reported cracked or broken windowpanes so far, and many windows of businesses in New Zebedee were shattered. However, the *Chronicle* chooses to look upon the bright side: trade will be profitable for glaziers this yuletide season.

It is believed the meteor plummeted to earth somewhere south of New Zebedee. No doubt it would be an object of scientific inquiry in the event of its discovery.

If any of our gentle readers, on a woodland ramble, should descry a smouldering crater, the *Chronicle* will gladly pay that person ten dollars to be led to the site of impact. Tell only the *Chronicle*, however. If you whisper the news to the disgruntled goddess Diana, she very well might smite you with a curse.

"Huh," said Rose Rita. "They didn't take it very seriously at the time, did they?"

"Maybe the story's written that way because the reporter was glad no one actually got hurt," replied Lewis. "I guess something like a meteorite smashing to the earth would be pretty scary. People would naturally feel relieved after it ended and they were all right."

"Maybe so," agreed Rose Rita. They turned more pages, and in the obituary column for Wednesday, they found an entry for Jebediah Clabbernong. It didn't say very much: "Jebediah Clabbernong, farmer, passed from this life suddenly about midnight on 21st December. Services will be private."

That was it. The rest of the December papers had no stories about either meteors or Clabbernongs. Lewis brooded as Rose Rita closed the big volume. Something was rattling around in his memory. "Hey," he said. "Isn't 21st December the shortest day of the year?"

"Right," said Rose Rita. "It's the solstice, the first day of winter. That's the shortest day and the longest night of the whole year. And tomorrow's the first day of summer, which has the longest day and the shortest night of the year. So what?"

"Maybe it means something," said Lewis. "It could be that old Jebediah did some magic that called the meteor to earth that night. You know, witches and wizards can cast their strongest spells only on certain days of the year. Uncle Jonathan can eclipse the moon, but not just at any old time. All the stars have to be in the right places. And even then, the eclipse isn't a real one. It's only good for about a square mile or so."

Rose Rita tapped her fingers on the library table. "You may be right," she said slowly. "I don't know how you'd find out for sure, though. I mean, if you don't want to check with your uncle or with Mrs Zimmermann—"

"Gosh, no," said Lewis quickly. "They might think I'm meddling just by reading all these old newspaper stories."

Rose Rita pushed her chair away from the table. "OK. I think you're probably mistaken, but I know this whole thing is really bothering you. How about this: why don't we go check out that old farm?"

Lewis felt as if his stomach had suddenly frozen. "I—I don't know," he stammered. "It—it's way out of town, and, and—"

"We could get there on our bikes in a couple of hours," coaxed Rose Rita. "We've gone that far plenty of times. If we left early, like at seven in the morning, we could be there no later than nine or nine-thirty. Maybe we could go on Saturday. That'd give us a couple of days to get ready for the trip. Then we could poke around at the farm for a few hours, have a picnic, and ride back, with nobody the wiser."

Rose Rita was right. Still, Lewis's chest felt as if a giant hand were gripping him, squeezing the breath from his lungs. After the awful things he had overheard his uncle say, he dreaded even the thought of that sinister, blighted farm. "Wh-what d-do you think we'd f-find there?" he faltered, stalling for time.

"The place where the meteorite hit," replied Rose Rita. "Or a book of magic spells. Or a

Secret Decoder Ring. Who knows? One thing's for sure, though. We won't find a single solitary thing unless we try."

Lewis swallowed, trying to gulp down a painful lump in his throat. "Are you sure we should go? It's a horrible place. Aren't you scared?" he croaked.

Rose Rita gave him a sickly smile. "I'm scared, all right," she confessed. "But it will be in the daytime, we'll be together, and we'll run like rabbits if anything bizarre happens. I promise."

Lewis's head spun. More than anything, he wanted to reassure himself that his uncle loved him and trusted him and would never send him away. This scheme of Rose Rita's might help him to do that—or it might cause everything to come crashing down, like the grotesque cage in his nightmare. Lewis wished he had more determination and gumption. He wished he could act decisively, like Rose Rita, and not dither and worry about everything before it happened.

He forced himself to speak calmly. "OK. I'll go. But if anything happens—"

"We run," promised Rose Rita. "Like rabbits."

"Like rabbits," Lewis repeated, and so it was settled.

CHAPTER FIVE

At dinner on Wednesday evening Lewis asked his uncle if he and Rose Rita could go for a long bike ride. Jonathan, who had been serving himself some mashed potatoes, paused. "Why, I suppose that would be all right," he said. "Better now than in July, when the temperature is guaranteed to hit a hundred and fifty and you could fry up a bacon-and-egg breakfast on the pavement." He spooned the mashed potatoes into his plate. "And speaking of food, I'll buy some sandwich fixings. No sense in you two starving to death out in the country-side."

So Lewis and Rose Rita planned their expedition for the following Saturday. However, on Friday, Lewis woke to find the morning stormy. Low, ragged grey clouds whipped through the sky, fitful gusts of wind whistled in the eaves, and hard, brief spatters of rain struck the windows. Lewis secretly felt a deep relief. If this kind of weather held, then the bike trip was off, and he really didn't want to go.

Towards noon a thunderstorm broke, the kind that Uncle Jonathan called a "frog choker." Sheets of lead-coloured rain drummed on the roof. Crackling streaks of lightning sizzled and flashed, and booms of thunder rattled the windows and made the floor vibrate. For about three minutes a hailstorm pounded New Zebedee. There were so many round pellets of ice the size of marbles that bounced and cracked on the ground that the yard almost looked as if there had been a June snow. The hail ended abruptly, but the rain, lightning, and thunder grew even worse.

Jonathan sat in the study with an unlit pipe clenched in his teeth. His attention was focused on some book of magic. Usually thunderstorms scared Lewis, but this one seemed a deliverance. He went to the staircase in the south wing of the mansion and sat on the landing, staring at the changeable stained-glass window. It was no longer a scarlet warning sign. Instead it showed a simple white farmhouse at the end of a yellow lane leading through green fields. A white bird flew over the roof, the only object in a cheerful blue sky.

Lightning made the oval picture flare bright now and then. Despite the storm, the peaceful scene the window pictured gave Lewis a feeling of serenity. Maybe he was all worked up over nothing. Since the prospect of a trip out to the Clabbernong farm seemed remote, he felt as if a heavy weight had been taken off his shoulders.

A deafening crash of thunder made even the stairs shake. The electric lights flickered to a dull orange, then went out. Instantly, the staircase became a gloomy shaft of darkness. Lewis hurriedly sprang to his feet and dashed up to the second floor. He rushed into his room and threw himself on his bed. One of his aunts had always told him you were safe in a thunderstorm if you were lying on a feather bed.

Lewis did not know if his mattress had feathers or foam rubber or lobster whiskers inside. He didn't even know if what his aunt said was true or just one of her superstitions.

But superstition or fact, Lewis felt a little more secure in his bed. He lay there while the storm raged outside. He glanced at his clock. With a strange sensation of revulsion, he saw that the iron rivet once more shimmered with those ghostly colours. In fact, the colours were brighter than ever. Each time a bolt of lightning flashed, they flared up, as if the electricity in the air gave them more energy. Looking at the rivet, Lewis could hardly tell that it was made of solid iron. Its surface was a swirling, flowing, pulsing mass of colour.

Lewis opened the drawer of his night table. It held lots of junk: old playing cards, some *Monopoly* tokens, a few photos, and other odds and ends. Gingerly, using just the tip of his finger, Lewis flicked at the rivet until it rolled into the drawer. Then he slammed the drawer shut. He looked fearfully at the tip of his right forefinger, wondering if it would start to glow. The strange tints and hues on the rivet apparently were not catching, because his fingertip just looked like skin.

Not long after that, the power came back on. The storm blew over, retreating towards the east with some last bellowed threats of thunder and a few spiteful lashings of rain. Lewis knelt at his window and looked out. The sky was clearing, with patches of blue already breaking through the clouds. A few sodden leaves stuck to his window, and he could hear water dripping from the chestnut tree in the front yard. Still, the storm had ended.

By dinner that evening the sky was clear. The weatherman on television predicted a warm, bright Saturday and Sunday. Lewis knew that his and Rose Rita's trip was still on, and his heart felt heavy inside his chest. That night he slept fitfully. Once more he had strange, terrifying dreams, though he could not exactly remember them when he woke up at four minutes past three o'clock. He just had the impression that something vast and without pity had been chasing him. And what about the rivet? What was it doing?

With mingled dread and anticipation, Lewis opened the drawer of his bedside table. Nothing glowed inside. The rivet was just a three-inch piece of iron. Lewis closed the drawer again and dropped off to sleep.

The alarm went off at six-thirty, its metallic clatter jarring Lewis from a deep, dreamless doze. He flailed out and switched the clock off, then sat on the edge of his bed, woozy from his broken sleep. Little patches of sticky gunk made his eyelids feel gluey. He got up, went to the bathroom, and splashed water on his face.

Then he plodded back and peeped out the window. The day was fair. Rose Rita would be there in twenty-five minutes.

Lewis got dressed and went quietly downstairs, in case his uncle was still asleep. Before he reached the bottom of the stairs, though, Lewis smelled bacon. He found Uncle Jonathan and Mrs Zimmermann in the kitchen, both of them wearing aprons and bustling around the stove. "Good morning," Uncle Jonathan said. "Before you set off on your voyage of exploration, would you like one scrambled egg or two?"

Lewis had two, as well as a couple of pieces of thick-cut bacon and two wonderful slices of sourdough toast, spread with country butter and Mrs Zimmermann's own tangy apple jam. Mrs Zimmermann said, "I knew that Jonathan's idea of making a sandwich is simply to slap some meat between two pieces of bread, so I came over and put your picnic together. You have two sandwiches each. I've also put in a couple of my extra-fudge brownies and two of my special dill pickles. That recipe for pickles won a blue ribbon at the Capharnaum County Fair, so you eat them with reverence!"

With a smile Lewis promised that he and Rose Rita would. He packed all the food into his bike's saddlebags. "What are you going to drink?" asked Jonathan, standing at the back door.

"We'll stop at a filling station somewhere and buy two sodas," replied Lewis.

Jonathan reached into his pocket and pulled out his fat old brown leather wallet. He took two one-dollar bills from it. "Here you are," he said. "And you may keep the change. Lewis, Mrs Zimmermann and I have a few errands to run, so I may not be home until three or a little later. Tell Rose Rita that if she wants to eat dinner with us, Haggy's volunteered to cook."

Behind him, in the kitchen, Mrs Zimmermann snorted pertly. "Good thing for you I have! The only real nourishment you boys ever get comes from my cooking!"

"I'll invite Rose Rita to dinner," said Lewis, and he wheeled his bike around to the front.

He bounced it carefully down the steps to the pavement, and a few seconds later, Rose Rita appeared, pumping the pedals of her bike hard as she pulled up the hill.

She came to a stop, huffing and puffing. "Ready?" she asked, leaning on one foot.

Lewis nodded glumly. "I guess so."

"Then let's go." She turned, and they rolled down the slope without even pedalling, and headed downtown. It was barely seven o'clock, and New Zebedee was just waking up. Few cars were moving, though they saw the milkman making his rounds. They rode through town and then turned south, with the sun on their left. Away to the right, their shadows, long in the morning light, flickered along the edge of the road and out across dew-covered meadows.

By seven-thirty they reached Wilder Creek Road, pedalling silently in single file, with Rose Rita in the lead. Once or twice a pickup truck rattled past, full of sweet corn, tomatoes, and other produce the farmer was taking into New Zebedee to sell.

In a way Lewis found the trip very pleasant. The weather was exactly right, not too warm and just cool enough. Robins and mockingbirds sang jaunty morning songs from the chestnut and oak trees they passed. Lewis began to get that second-wind feeling, the sense that he could go on like this forever, knees pumping, heart pounding steadily, and not ever get tired.

Rose Rita pulled off the road just short of the new bridge. Lewis stopped too and rolled his bike up beside hers. "They've almost finished," he said. All the iron that had made up the frame of the old bridge had been taken down. Only the two heavy side supports and four upright piers remained. A big truck with a long bed had been loaded up with black girders, and it sagged under their weight.

As Lewis and Rose Rita stared at the sad ruin of the old bridge, a maroon Ford pulled up and stopped near a bulldozer. A chunky red-faced man got out. He wore a blue-and-white checked shirt, faded jeans, and scuffed brown work boots. A droopy, bushy black moustache hid his mouth, and although the top of his head was bald, big poofs of black hair clung to the sides, just behind his ears. "Hiya," he said, waving in a friendly way. "Quite a thunder-boomer yesterday, huh?"

"Pretty bad storm," Rose Rita agreed. "Are you working on the bridge?"

The man had reached into his Ford for a clipboard and white safety helmet. He slammed the car door shut and said, "Well, now, I'd say the work *on* the bridge is just about over. She's a real beauty, huh? We're gonna pull up the roots of the old one, and then I guess our job is done."

"When will you finish?" asked Rose Rita.

The workman looked at what remained of the bridge. He scratched his nose thoughtfully. "Hmm. We're behind schedule—that's why we're working on Saturday—but it won't be long. Take just a little more time to get the last parts up. We'll be done by next weekend, probably. Might take a couple of sticks of dynamite to loosen these old pilings. But after, say, a week from today, you'll never know there used to be an old bridge here."

"What happens to the iron?" asked Lewis.

"Huh?" The man scratched his bald head, then clapped his helmet on. "Dunno, sonny. Never thought about it, to tell ya the truth. I s'pose the company sells it for scrap, something like that. Tell ya one thing, though: this is good iron. Sturdy and not a speck of rust anywhere. They don't make it like this any more."

"I guess not," said Lewis.

A truck full of workmen bounced off on to the shoulder of the road on the other side of the bridge, and the man began to yell for them to get busy. Rose Rita rode her bike across the new bridge, with Lewis right behind her. For nearly an hour they pedalled through the countryside, neither saying anything. At the little crossroads with the cannon, the church, and the general store, they stopped to buy sodas and use the bathroom. Luckily, the store had just opened. A yawning man wished them a good morning and sold them two bottles of cola.

By then it was past eight-thirty. They got to the old Clabbernong farm at fifteen minutes past nine. Once a dirt drive had run down from the farmhouse to the road. The driveway had become a rutted, rough track too cut by washouts for them to ride across. They got off and rolled their bikes up to the dilapidated farmhouse.

The second-floor windows were choked with fallen timbers and twisted, rusty pieces of the collapsed tin roof. All the glass in the first-floor windows was long gone, leaving gaping holes into the darkness. Close to the house, the nauseating smell lingered, though after the rain it didn't seem as strong as it had been. Lewis felt a strange disorientation. For a moment he could not put his finger on the cause, but then he whispered, "Rose Rita, listen."

Rose Rita stopped. "I don't hear anything."

"That's what I mean," said Lewis. "All the time we were riding, I could hear birds singing or katydids chirping. But here there's nothing."

"Creepy," agreed Rose Rita. They had reached the sagging farmhouse porch. "Let's leave our bikes here," she suggested.

Lewis put down the kickstand on his bike. "I don't think we should go inside," he said, staring through the open doorway of the old house. Lazy dust motes floated there in a shaft of sunlight, but everything around it was dark. "This place looks like it could collapse any second. And the smell is terrible."

Rose Rita nodded. "It's like old mouldy food and dead mice and rotten tomatoes—"

"Please," groaned Lewis. "I don't want to be sick."

They prowled around the side of the house. As Uncle Jonathan had said, the grass was not only dead but somehow almost crystallised. It crunched under their feet, turning into gritty powder. Behind the house they found a swaybacked barn, its tin roof intact. The boards were blackened with age and warped from the weather. Off to the left Lewis saw a crumbling redbrick well, which rose about as high as his waist. The windlass was still in place, wound with a decayed rope. A bashed-in old bucket stood on the well's lip, though it had rusted to a solid orange-red.

"I don't see anything," said Lewis in a timid voice. "I don't think there's anything to find."

"Let's look past the barn," replied Rose Rita. "Mrs Zimmermann said the meteorite crashed down somewhere beyond it."

Unwillingly, Lewis followed her. A few old fence posts leaned crazily this way and that, connected by rusty strands of barbed wire. Dead weeds stood at stiff attention in the abandoned pasture. Whenever Lewis or Rose Rita brushed against them, they dissolved into grit.

"Why hasn't the weather destroyed all this stuff?" asked Lewis. "You'd think that rain and hail and wind would have—"

He broke off at a squeak from Rose Rita, a few steps ahead of him. "Here it is," she said, standing at the crest of a low hill. Lewis toiled up after her and stared down into a bowl-shaped crater. "It's not smouldering, though," added Rose Rita. "I wonder if the *Chronicle* would still pay me the ten dollars."

The crater, if that's what it was, was bare. No grass grew around or in it. Some water had collected—just a small puddle. The sides were mud, but mud that already was drying and cracked. Lewis guessed the pit was ten feet across at the top, fifteen feet deep, and tapered down until at the bottom it was only a couple of feet in diameter. The sides sloped steeply down. "Now that we've found it," said Lewis, "what are we supposed to do? I'm not going to dig around in that glop, if that's what you're thinking."

"I don't believe we'd find anything anyway," said Rose Rita. "At least we know where the meteorite hit, though. OK, let's head to someplace less stinky, and we can have our sandwiches and decide what to do next."

They were passing the barn when, with a yelp, Rose Rita pitched forwards and vanished! For a stunned moment Lewis thought she had pulled off some magic trick. Then he heard her terrified wail, "Get me out of here! Help!"

Lewis saw that a hole had opened in the earth, and Rose Rita had dropped inside. He could see the broken ends of rotted planks. Lewis fell on to his stomach and crept to the edge of the hole. Looking down, he had a glimpse of old brick walls. Sunlight streamed into the darkness, and in it, Rose Rita's pale face was looking up at him. She was only a couple of feet below him.

"I can get you," he said, reaching down. "Grab my hands!"

Rose Rita was panting. "This is an old storm cellar," she said, her voice panicky. "Wait a minute—here, take this. Hurry! Take it!" She thrust something into Lewis's hands, and he hauled it out. It was a red cedar box about the size of a cigar humidor. "Now pull me out!" Rose Rita screamed. "I can't stand this!"

Lewis knew Rose Rita's suffocating fear of tight spaces was overpowering her. He dropped the wooden box and thrust his hands down to her again. He felt her grab his wrists, and he hauled back. Rose Rita's head and shoulders popped out of the hole. She let go with her left hand and pushed down against the ground. With her shoving and Lewis pulling, somehow they hoisted her free.

Rose Rita could not stop shivering. "Ugh! It was so d-dark down th-there, and it smelled like it had been closed off for a h-hundred years!"

Lewis heard something behind him. A dry, rustling sound, like crackly old paper being slowly crunched. A hoarse, wheezing *hhaahhhh* sound, as if something were breathing its last. Rose Rita looked over his shoulder towards the barn. She clapped a hand over her mouth, her eyes wide and filled with terror.

Feeling as if his heart were climbing right into his mouth, Lewis forced himself to turn.

Something was trying to walk from the ruined old barn.

Something big and grey and lurching.

Once it might have been a horse.

Now it was a lumpy, dry, silvery shape. As its misshapen foreleg tried to take a step, chunks of grainy flesh fell away in a shower of flakes. The smooth brittle bones splintered. The mouth parted and horrible moaning sounds came out. The eye sockets were empty, but to Lewis they seemed to plead for an ending—for death.

Afterwards, he could not even remember starting to run. All he knew was that he was rushing to their bikes, dragging Rose Rita by the hand. They had promised each other they would run like rabbits, and Lewis certainly did. He did not even notice that Rose Rita had picked up the wooden box.

"Look!" shouted Rose Rita at the corner of the house.

The shambling monstrosity had reached the old storm cellar. The wood gave way beneath it. With a final despairing bawl, it fell into the pit. An explosion of dust boiled up.

And then, somehow, they were both on their bikes, pedalling for their lives, riding away from the farm and its terrible secrets.

CHAPTER SIX

Lewis and Rose Rita rode their bikes all the way back to New Zebedee without even pausing for breath. By the time they rolled to a stop in East End Park, both of them were gasping, and Lewis's legs felt dead with fatigue. They had been going without a break for miles, and he was worn out.

They let their bikes clatter to the ground and sat on the grass, panting. Lewis's lungs were burning, and each gulp of air didn't seem enough to keep him going. At last Rose Rita got to her feet, almost staggering. She jerked her head towards a bench under a tall fir, and Lewis forced himself to stand up and follow her. He collapsed on to the bench. "Let's eat," said Rose Rita. "It's already noon."

"In a minute," replied Lewis. "I'm gonna die if I have to move again. I have to rest."

"I'll get the sandwiches," said Rose Rita.

The two of them munched their sandwiches and sipped their warm sodas while people walked past. Lewis barely noticed what he was eating. That was a shame, because Mrs Zimmermann had really outdone herself with roast beef, sweet onions, cheese, creamy mild mustard, lettuce, and tomatoes. But Lewis might as well have been swallowing cardboard on whole wheat.

A few other people came to sit in the park or strolled past, but no one paid them much attention. Around midday, lots of people ate sandwiches in the park. Lewis felt strange. Not because anything in the park was odd—far from it. No, the park, the passers-by, the cars on the street, the warm sun, all these were *normal.* So normal that they made everything that had happened at the farm seem like one more nightmare. If only Lewis could have awakened from it, he would have been grateful.

Unfortunately, he knew that what had happened was real—just as real as Mrs Zimmermann's crunchy dill pickles. When Lewis and Rose Rita had finished their lunches, he balled up the wax-paper wrappers and tossed them into a trash can. He put their empty soda bottles in his bike saddlebags because he could get back deposit money for them. "OK," said Rose Rita, opening her own saddlebag. From inside it she took the wooden box she had found at the farm. "I guess I feel up to it now. Let's see what this booby prize can be."

She turned the box around and over, trying to see how it opened. To Lewis the container looked like a solid piece of wood, though he remembered that something had clunked inside it when he had taken it from Rose Rita. Finally, Rose Rita found a tiny crack, no thicker than a hair. She tried to work her fingernail into it, without success.

Lewis reached into his jeans pocket and found his Boy Scout pocketknife. "Here," said Lewis, holding it out to Rose Rita. "Try this."

Rose Rita opened the penknife blade and slipped the tip into the crack. Prying into the seam, she forced the box lid open at last. It swung on a hidden hinge. Inside the box lay a book about nine inches high and six inches wide, not very thick. The binding was a faded pale green cloth, with badly scuffed oxblood-red leather reinforcements on the spine and corners. To Lewis the volume looked like an old-fashioned ledger. An aroma of cedar, clean and sharp, drifted from the box as Rose Rita took the book out.

"Well?" asked Lewis impatiently. "Does it have a title, or—"

"Keep your shirt on," murmured Rose Rita. "Let's see." She carefully opened the book, and Lewis could see it was indeed a ledger, the pages marked with faint blue ruled lines. The old leaves were shiny, although they had faded to a dull tan. On the first page, inscribed in a spidery handwriting in ink that had aged to the colour of chocolate, was the title:

MYSTIC JOURNAL OF JEBEDIAH CLABBERNONG

"Well," said Rose Rita, "at least we know this thing belonged to Old Creepy. Let's see what he has to say." She turned to the next page. For a moment both of them just stared at it, baffled. To Lewis's disappointment, the book didn't make any sense at all. Page after page was filled with fussy little sketches of stars, mermaids, anchors, weird-looking flowers, and lumpy human and animal figures, with some annotations in the same handwriting as the title:

Ffp. in 2 segs., w/d.k.a., prep'd accd to Rule of Yog.
Tried 9th incnt. from N'con, tr. from Fr. copy. Rslt nil. No good w/o Elem. of Salamander. Mst. chk in Josephus or clavicle.

voorish sign, midnight, on stony height. partial manifst. poss. G-O-O. Or Spirit? Or Elemental?

Lewis sat shaking his head as Rose Rita turned the pages. Then, halfway through the book—about fifty pages in—the writing suddenly settled into a diary format. The first entry read:

March 1860. Calculations and great disappointment. Red Star will not appear for hundreds of years. I must not die before opening the Portal! I must try the Rite of Kl'ash-t'un. Perhaps I may pull a fragment from the comet to Earth ahead of time. Even that might suffice. Great power required. What would it take from me? Health? Sanity? Worth any risk!

Lewis frowned as they read other entries, usually separated by gaps of weeks or months. Jebediah spent lots of time wondering where he could find things:

Must read the Seven Rituals in the Book of Nameless Horrors. Only copy in country is in Massachusetts. Must travel there.

Later, he had written:

Oh, for a complete edition of the Names of the Dead Ones! It maddens me to be so close and not have the great key!

In June of 1865 he had written:

Have performed the awful Rite of Kl'ash-t'un, to the Rule of Three, and Six, and Nine, for nine days, eighteen days, and twenty-seven days. Success. Exhaustion, prostration, slept for three days, very weak. How long to wait? Ten years? Twenty-five? I am in middle age! Must live until Rite is fulfilled. Perhaps a sacrifice to extend my years.

And then, six months later:

It is done. Nephew and his wife. Burial tomorrow. What of grandnephew? Only relative. Orphanage? No. I have desired an apprentice. Only two years old. Much time to bend and twist him to my will.

Rose Rita looked up from the book, her expression appalled. "He killed his own nephew and his wife! Somehow he sacrificed them both so he would live long enough to see the fragment of the Red Star."

"The meteor," put in Lewis. "The paper said it was as red as blood."

"So it took twenty years to get to Earth," said Rose Rita.

Lewis slowly said, "And the two-year-old grandnephew would have been Elihu Clabbernong." He looked around, but no one was anywhere close to them. "My gosh, Rose Rita, Jebediah Clabbernong was using his terrible magic! We've got to give this journal to Uncle Jonathan!"

Rose Rita shook her head. "Let's finish

reading it first. The more we know, the better off we are."

They pieced together some faint understanding of what Jebediah Clabbernong had been trying to do. Lewis was not clear on any of the details, but Jebediah had believed that before humans existed on Earth, a race of creatures he called the Great Old Ones had lived here. These beings practised some kind of diabolical sorcery, and because of that, some great power had banished them to another dimension.

Lewis got the impression that the Great Old Ones were monsters, not even remotely shaped like humans. Though the book did not really describe them, it left images of wet, slimy things in Lewis's mind, squids and slugs and starfish. Some of the Great Old Ones were always trying to break through into our dimension to reclaim the Earth as their own. Others had flown away to the depths of outer space. After humans spread over the Earth, most people believed the Great Old Ones had been some kind of demon. Others thought they were only myths and legends.

But a few people, like Jebediah, worshipped them as gods. Jebediah believed that if he could "open the Portal" and let at least one of the Great Old Ones through, they would destroy humanity and become lords of Earth again. As for Jebediah, he would be changed in body into a Great Old One himself. Then he would have enormous power and would never die. He bent his whole life to that cause.

Towards the end of the journal, Jebediah was becoming more and more angry and frantic. "*I age! I age! Half blind, weak in arms and legs! How much longer can I endure?*" he had written. And "*Curse this Earth! Curse its people, all of them merely crawling worms! Just let me live until the Red Star lights all the heavens and the time is right for the Opening of the Way!*"

And, at last, the final entry, dated 1st December 1885. It was simple and short and chilling: "*It comes.*"

After that, only blank pages remained.

Rose Rita closed the book. "Twenty days later

the meteorite hit," she said in a low voice. "And old spooky Jebediah died."

"Wh-what if he didn't?" asked Lewis. "I m-mean, wh-what if Elihu *thought* he was dead, but the old man really b-became—became—" He could not even finish the thought.

Rose Rita looked sick. "What if he—he became like that—that animal we saw?" she asked. For a moment she didn't say anything, and when she spoke again, her voice was a whisper. "He was nutty enough to try that, if he thought it would let him hang on until the Red Star came and he could open his crazy Portal."

Lewis took a long, shaky breath. "I don't understand. People must have gone out to that place since 1885," he said. "People are curious. *Someone* must have visited the farm after Jebediah died or disappeared. How come they didn't see that—that creature?"

Rose Rita said thoughtfully, "Maybe it wasn't there then. Or maybe it was just a pile of dry dust in the corner of a barn stall. If what Jebediah wrote was accurate, the Red Star should be showing up any year now. Maybe as it comes close to Earth, it's bringing the creatures to—not to life, but to some kind of awareness and movement. Maybe—maybe old Jebediah is about to rise from the dead—" She broke off, closing her eyes.

"We've got to give this book to Uncle Jonathan," said Lewis again. "But if we do, he's going to know I've been meddling."

Rose Rita bit her lip. "I think we can fix that. Have you got any money on you?"

Lewis took the change out of his pocket and counted it. "I've got a dollar and eighty cents."

"Good," Rose Rita said. "Go over to the dime store and buy a pad, a pencil, and a ruler. Then come back."

Lewis hurried across the street and soon returned with a yellow writing pad, a wooden ruler, and a pencil. He sharpened the pencil with his Boy Scout knife. The cedar aroma nearly made him gag because it reminded him of the book. When the pencil was sharp, Rose Rita took it from him. "If you print in block letters, using a ruler as a guide, nobody can recognise your handwriting," she explained.

Lewis blinked. "Huh? How'd you know that?"

"I heard it on *Philip Marlowe*," answered Rose Rita. That was a detective show she really liked. "OK. Let's figure out what we ought to say."

They worked out the note, and then, carefully, Rose Rita printed the message on a sheet of paper. When she finished, both she and Lewis read it over:

DEAR MR BARNAVELT,
THIS JOURNAL MIGHT HELP YOU UNDERSTAND JEBEDIAH CLABBERNONG. PLEASE DO WHATEVER YOU CAN. TIME IS RUNNING OUT.
    SIGNED, A FRIEND

Rose Rita had wanted to sign the note "The Hidden Avenger," but Lewis talked her out of that. "It may do the trick," Lewis said. "Now what?"

Rose Rita folded the note and put it inside the book. "We leave the box on your doorstep and make ourselves scarce. Your uncle said he'd be away from home until about three o'clock. It's not even two yet. We'll drop off the box, come back to town, and not go back to your house until about four o'clock. Your uncle will assume we're just getting back from our bike ride. He won't have any idea who left the package."

After all their exertion, their legs were aching. They rode to the base of the hill. They were too tired to pedal up, so they walked their bikes to 100 High Street.

Rose Rita waited on the pavement. Feeling like a burglar, Lewis went to the front door and tried the letterbox. The wooden box just barely fit through. He heard it clonk to the floor, and then he hurried back to join Rose Rita. They went over to Spruce Street Park, near the town waterworks, and rested in the shade for over an hour. For a while they didn't talk very much. Rose Rita's experience in the old storm cellar had really shaken her. Finally, she stretched and looked around. "I wonder if that hole in the ground might have been old Creepy Clabbernong's secret magical workshop."

"What did it look like?" asked Lewis.

Rose Rita made a face. "Like the inside of a burial vault. The walls were brick and the floor was dirt. One wall had a shelf built into it, and the box was on that."

"Did you see any magical stuff?" asked Lewis. "Like black candles and swords and such?"

Rose Rita shook her head. She hugged herself, as if the memory still tormented her. "All I saw was just the little room under the ground."

"Then," said Lewis, "I think it was just a storm cellar." Tornadoes weren't common in Capharnaum County, but every so often one hit. Most of the farmers in the area had dug out storm cellars where their families could ride out a really bad twister. "You know," continued Lewis, "I'll bet you that old Jebediah didn't trust his grandnephew. Mrs Zimmermann told us that Elihu burned all his granduncle's papers.

But I'll bet that he didn't even know about that journal, or about where Jebediah hid it. It could be that Jebediah didn't—what was it that he wrote? Didn't bend and twist Elihu to his will, after all."

Rose Rita grimaced. "If that was so, I'd think Elihu would have done a better job of getting rid of Jebediah and all his works."

"He tried his best," Lewis pointed out. "He built that bridge. And he put meteor stuff in the iron. He—"

Rose Rita gave him a sharp glance. "What's the matter? You look like a goose just walked over your grave."

Lewis forced himself to speak. His voice sounded odd and strangled even to himself: "Rose Rita," he whispered. "What if something came to Earth inside that meteorite? What if the meteorite was kind of like an egg?"

Rose Rita stared at him. "What if one of the Great Old Ones hatched out of it, you mean?"

Lewis murmured, "The journal said that some of them went to outer space. What if one of them came *back*? And what if the meteorite was made of the only stuff in the universe that could contain it?"

Slowly, Rose Rita said, "Then that might be why Elihu melted the meteorite into the iron. He wasn't trying to keep the ghost of his uncle from getting him at all. He was trying to keep something else from crossing the creek."

"And now," faltered Lewis, "it will be able to cross anytime it wants to!"

Miles away, Uncle Jonathan and Mrs Zimmermann stood on the hill overlooking Wilder Creek and its new bridge. The workmen below were busily preparing to remove one of the old iron bridge pilings. A crane towered high in the air, with a steel cable attached to the head of the piling. Everyone had retreated. A workman hooked some wires to a plunger and then signalled. The foreman waved his arm, and the workman pushed the handle of the plunger down. It set off dynamite under the water. A fountain of bright white spray shot up, and a moment later the sharp explosion sounded. The piling swayed.

The creek boiled with scummy yellow bubbles. Even at this distance, Jonathan and Mrs Zimmermann could hear cries of disgust from the workmen. A moment later the breeze brought a sickening stench to their nostrils too.

CHAPTER SEVEN

"Florence," Uncle Jonathan whispered, "I'm very, very worried."

Mrs Zimmermann put her hand on his arm. She did not say anything. But she shook her head slowly, as if she were just as concerned as her friend.

When Lewis returned to 100 High Street, he found that Uncle Jonathan was back home too. His uncle said nothing about finding the wooden box with its mysterious journal. Rose Rita came over for dinner, and she kept a sharp eye on Mrs Zimmermann. Neither of the two adults gave the least hint that they had found the journal.

Later, Rose Rita and Lewis had a hasty, whispered conversation before Rose Rita left for home. "Keep an eye on them," urged Rose Rita. "I want to be sure they got the book."

"It didn't walk off," responded Lewis. "Uncle Jonathan must've picked it up with the rest of the mail."

"Watch anyway," said Rose Rita, and she left.

Though he felt like a spy in his own home, Lewis did settle in to watch his uncle and Mrs Zimmermann.

Nothing happened until the following Wednesday. At lunchtime, Uncle Jonathan said, "Lewis, why don't you and Rose Rita go to the movies this evening? There's a new western on."

"I don't like cowboys too much," hedged Lewis.

His uncle smiled. "Well, I'm having some people over, and I'm afraid you'd be bored out of your mind here. At least it will be cool in the theatre." When Lewis still looked doubtful, his uncle added, "Tell you what. You go to the movies, and one day soon we'll have Rose Rita over and I'll put on a private show about the Battle of the Nile, or maybe Trafalgar." Lewis knew that Jonathan meant he would cast one of his wonderful illusion spells. They were just like Technicolor movies, except they were three-dimensional and you could actually take part in them.

Reluctantly, Lewis agreed to go to the movies. But when he called Rose Rita, she said, "This is it. I'd bet that the Capharnaum County Magicians Society is meeting at your house this evening. We have to find out for sure if your uncle found the book. Think of a way."

Immediately, Lewis thought of one possibility. The house at 100 High Street had an extra-special feature: a secret passageway. It wasn't very long, and it wasn't even very practical. The secret passage led from behind a cupboard in the kitchen to a space behind a bookcase in the study. No one knew why it had been built in the first place, but it was an ideal spot for two snooping kids to hide. The trick would be getting into the passage without being caught.

That afternoon Jonathan gave Lewis five dollars. "You can get a hamburger and soda and still have enough left for the movie," he said. "Since you'll be coming back after dark, wear something light coloured and be sure to walk facing the traffic."

It seemed to Lewis that his uncle was being especially fussy. Usually he trusted Lewis to remember things like that, for Jonathan knew his nephew had a lot of common sense. Rose Rita came over at five o'clock. Mrs Zimmermann and Uncle Jonathan were puttering around in the kitchen, making hors d'oeuvres for the guests. Lewis called, "We're going now!"

"Be careful, you two!" his uncle shouted back. "Have a good time."

But instead of leaving the house, Lewis and Rose Rita ducked into the study. The one tricky thing about the secret passage was that, at the study end, the latch was on the outside, not the inside. Lewis released the catch and swung a large section of the built-in bookcase open. It moved silently on unseen hinges, and Lewis and Rose Rita walked into the passageway.

It was cramped and dark inside. As Lewis pulled the bookcase section back into place, he heard Rose Rita begin to gasp for air. He remembered how she was afraid of closed-in spaces. "Are you OK?" he asked.

Rose Rita took several deep breaths. "I will be. This isn't so bad. It's more like a little room than—than anything else. And I can see light around the edges of the door."

For a few minutes they stood shoulder to shoulder. Gradually Rose Rita's breathing calmed down. Now and then she looked through a small peephole into the study. "Tell me when they show up," said Lewis.

"Are you sure they'll meet in there?" asked Rose Rita.

"That's where the Magicians Society always meets when they come over," said Lewis. "Are you all right now?"

Rose Rita shivered beside him. "I guess so. I still have the crazy feeling the walls are closing in, but it's OK as long as I'm not alone. It's not like being in a cave or a hole in the ground. Let's just settle down and not talk about it, OK?"

With nothing to do but wait, Lewis and Rose Rita sat on the floor, their backs against opposite walls of the passageway. "I wish we'd eaten first," whispered Lewis. "I'm going to be starving by the time everyone gets here."

Rose Rita moved in the darkness. "Hold out your hand."

Lewis did, and felt her put something into his open palm. "What's this?"

"It's a fudge bar," replied Rose Rita. "I figured we'd get hungry."

That was one of Lewis's favourite candy bars. He ate it. He and Rose Rita sat in the dark for what felt like hours. They heard scrapes and thuds as Uncle Jonathan dragged chairs into the study. At last they heard the sound of people talking. Rose Rita got up and surveyed the study through the peephole. "About two dozen people," she reported. "I see Mrs Jaeger, and there's Mr Plum. Looks like the meeting's about to start."

Lewis stood beside her, his ear close to the secret door. He heard his uncle say, "Thanks for coming, everybody. Before we start, Howard's asked me to remind you to pay your dues if you haven't already. Well, you know why we're all here. I wonder if any of you know who delivered this package last Saturday."

Voices murmured various versions of "No" and "What is it?"

"It seems to be a kind of sorcerous diary kept by Jebediah Clabbernong," said Uncle Jonathan. "Someone dropped it off here while I was out. There was a note, but it was signed only 'A Friend.'"

"What's in the book, Jonathan?" asked someone.

Jonathan said, "Florence and I have read through it a couple of times. We agreed you all should hear some of it. After the meeting, we'll ask a few of you to study this volume further. Florence, will you do the honours?"

Lewis heard Mrs Zimmermann clear her throat and then begin to read sections from the journal. When she finished, she said, "That's it. Does anyone know anything about this red star that he keeps mentioning?"

A man said, "It's a comet, Florence. It only visits the Earth once every thirteen or fourteen thousand years. It's supposed to be a source of energy for evil magicians. There's a passage in Flavius about it, and some hints in the Kabbala. I read in a magazine that astronomers recently spotted it deep in space."

"What about this business of the Great Old Ones?" asked Jonathan. "The only source of knowledge about them that I've ever heard of is the *Necronomicon*, and you all know how rare that dreadful book is. We'd never get our hands on a copy. Anything else?"

"The French aristocrat Comte D'Erlette has some writings about them," returned a woman's deep voice. "And there's that German book called *Unnameable Cults* or some such. They're supposed to be demonic creatures from another dimension, as far as I can tell."

"Of course," agreed Jonathan. "But what did old Jebediah have to do with them? And how does the meteorite figure in? Come to that, Walter, what have you found out about Jebediah's death back in 1885?"

A man answered, "Not very much. In 1885, Jebediah was a fairly elderly man. No one seems to know just how old he was, but he was at least seventy-five. He'd been in poor health for six months or so. He died on 21st December, the night the meteor hit. The coroner said he died of 'catalepsy,' which means some kind of paralysis. Stroke, I guess. His only heir was Elihu, who had the body cremated—which was hard to do back then, because it wasn't the custom. No one knows what happened to the old man's ashes."

"I can make a guess," said Mrs Zimmermann, "that Elihu scattered those ashes in the creek and later built the bridge over them. Either that, or he put them in a jar with some lead sinkers and tossed them into the creek. It's strangely deep at that point, you know—that's why it was odd that Elihu chose that place to build the bridge."

"What came to Earth in the meteorite?" someone else asked.

Lewis heard his uncle sigh. "That we don't know," he confessed. "Though it seems clear that Jebediah did call the meteorite down, somehow, and that *something* came to Earth along with it. But whether that something was an alien creature or a spirit, we haven't been able to learn. Florence and I tried to track down anything that Elihu left when he passed away, but we've had very little luck. He bequeathed all his money to various charities. The law firm in Kalamazoo that handled his estate refuses to comment on what happened to his personal papers."

"What law firm?" asked Mrs Jaeger, a pleasant, rather vague sorceress whose spells usually backfired.

"Moote, Mull, and Boyd," said Jonathan. "Unfortunately, Mr Moote is retired now, Mr Mull is dead, and I must say that Mr Boyd is about as talkative as the Sphinx."

"However," said Mrs Zimmermann, "I did drive over to Kalamazoo to have a look at the will—that's public record, you know. It's a perfectly ordinary legal document, stuffed with whereases and therefores and parties of the umpty parts. Except, that is, for one very strange paragraph." Lewis heard the rustle of paper. Mrs Zimmermann coughed and said, "I copied this down. See if you can make sense out of it. The paragraph says: 'Meanings may have other meanings. One thing I have learned is that the heart is the seat of the soul. The soul is the life. And the key to finding the life is, at the very bottom, a healthy heart.'" The paper rattled again, and Mrs Zimmermann said, "Well?"

The group muttered its puzzlement, and someone said, "Sounds like a health tip to me. Did Elihu die of a heart attack?"

"Pneumonia," Jonathan answered. "We're just as much in the dark as you are. Florence has made copies of that part of the will, and we'll hand them out. If anyone can think of a way to solve the riddle, or just prove that there's nothing to it, get in touch at once. Otherwise, let's all get busy."

"What do you want us to do?" asked someone.

"For one thing," said Mrs Zimmermann, "we need a subcommittee to study this journal. Howard, you and Walter know more about this kind of magic than anyone else here. If you two and Mildred could see what you can make of the book, we'd all appreciate a full report."

"For another," added Jonathan, "we need to have more information on this comet. When's it coming? What will its coming mean? What kind of influence will it have? I'll tackle that question. And finally, we have to keep up our watch on Wilder Creek. Florence and I are firmly convinced that something is stirring there, but we can't yet tell whether it's ghost or wizard or galloping woo-hoo. Florence can't detect any magic at work—"

"Then none is there," someone said. "I'd trust Florence with my life, where magic is concerned."

"So would I," responded Jonathan. "But let's be safe instead of sorry. Now, I'd suggest all of you with clairvoyance work out a rotation so we can keep tabs on the place twenty-four hours a day. Keep your crystal balls ready. I happen to know that on Friday the last piling of the old bridge comes out. Something may occur then. If it does, we need to know about it pronto."

Very little else happened. The meeting broke up into groups of people chatting and munching on snacks. With everyone still in the study, Lewis and Rose Rita slipped down the secret passage to the other end, came out in the kitchen, and took the back door outside. Dusk was falling already. They walked towards Rose Rita's house on Mansion Street.

"I guess our job is pretty clear too," said Rose Rita. "We have to help without getting caught."

"Haven't we done our part?" asked Lewis. "We turned the journal over to Uncle Jonathan."

"We still have things to do," insisted Rose Rita. "For one thing, I want to write down that puzzle from old Elihu's will while I can still remember it. Maybe we can figure that out. And we're going to be on watch just as much as the magicians are."

Lewis grunted. You couldn't argue with Rose Rita when she was in the mood to take charge. They reached her house. After Rose Rita had jotted down the words from Elihu Clabbernong's will, they went to the back yard, where they sat on patio furniture. From inside the Pottinger house came the sounds of a boxing match on the TV or the radio. Crickets chirped all around. The night grew darker and darker. Lewis lay back in his lawn chair and stared up at the sky. He could see a handful of stars strewn across the heavens. Somewhere among them might lurk the comet known as the Red Star. With every moment that passed, it was streaking closer to the

Earth. And who knew what disaster it might bring?

Not very far away, on a hill just outside New Zebedee, two other people were studying the stars. They were the old couple Mephistopheles and Ermine Moote, and they took turns bending over their telescope.

"It's coming faster than we thought, Mephisto," said the woman. "It will be visible to the naked eye any day now."

"No matter, no matter," the gnarled old man said in his raspy voice. "The cursed bridge is almost down. We will be free to act soon. Even if those busybodies in town find out about the comet, it will be too late! Once *he* is free, none will dare to oppose us!"

The woman backed away from the telescope, and the old man bent over the eyepiece with a gloating chuckle. The telescope mechanism ticked like a loud alarm clock. After a few moments the woman said, "Mephisto, while you were napping, Ernest Boyd telephoned from

Kalamazoo. He said the Zimmermann woman had been trying to find out if any of Jebediah's papers survived."

"Hah!" the old man cried out. "Much luck to her! What isn't burned is safely hidden away—hidden where no one, burglar, witch, or wizard, can find them!"

"One thing isn't," said the woman. "The will."

Mephistopheles Moote slowly straightened up from the eyepiece. "And what would she learn from the will, you fool? Just that Elihu frittered away his hard-earned money on orphans and widows! There's nothing in the will that can possibly hurt us!"

"Except the paragraph you never could understand," the woman said. "That part about the soul and the life and the heart."

With an annoyed grunt, Moote turned back to his telescope. "If she is smart enough to figure *that* rigmarole out, she is smarter than Mephistopheles P. Moote! I doubt that, but if she seems to be about to solve it—if she seems even close—we will take care of her, my dear."

He chuckled nastily. "Witches aren't immortal, you know. A witch can die."

The woman laughed too, a low, throaty sound in the dark. "Yes," she said. "A witch can certainly die."

CHAPTER EIGHT

Friday came and went peacefully. Lewis began to hope that everything might be all right, after all. On Saturday the newspaper reported that the last portion of the old bridge had been removed. Nothing, apparently, had happened to the workmen.

On Saturday too, a delivery truck pulled up in front of 100 High Street, and Uncle Jonathan signed for an assortment of mysterious packages, one of them taller than Lewis himself. Uncle Jonathan told Lewis to ask Rose Rita over if he wanted. He did, and only when she arrived did Uncle Jonathan consent to unpack all the boxes.

"Wow!" Lewis exclaimed when they had opened the tall one. It was a gleaming white tube with black metal fittings. Lewis knew what it was right away. "A telescope!"

"A good one, I hope," Uncle Jonathan stated. "I paid enough for it! It's an eight-inch reflector with a focal length of sixty-four inches. There's also a spotting scope, a pedestal mount with an electric motor, mounting rings, and eyepieces that will give you anywhere from thirty to five hundred magnification. I, uh, thought back-yard astronomy might be an interesting hobby."

They had a fine time assembling the instrument. As he and Uncle Jonathan were carefully attaching the tube to the mount, Lewis said, "I bet I know why you have to have a motor. The moon and stars and planets move, and the telescope has to move to keep them in sight."

"The Earth moves," corrected Rose Rita. "The stars *seem* to move because the Earth is rotating."

Uncle Jonathan had been kneeling as he finished the job. He stood up and took out a big bandana handkerchief to wipe his hands. He had a splotch of oil across his nose too that he didn't even notice. "There!" he said. "What a beauty! If it's clear tonight, we'll try it out." He took his gold pocket-watch from a bottom vest pocket and said, "We've taken up most of the afternoon with this! I wonder if Gravel Gertie is home. Rose Rita, call Mrs Zimmermann and ask her if she'd like to come over and see one of the wonders of the world."

Rose Rita ran to the phone. A minute later she came back and said, "She just got in from the library. She'll be right over."

"Good," said Uncle Jonathan. "Think she'll be impressed?"

"I think she'll be more impressed if you get the smudge off your nose," said Rose Rita.

Uncle Jonathan laughed and swabbed his face with the bandana. A moment later Mrs Zimmermann walked in without knocking. She was carrying a folder, and she shook her head and clucked her tongue when she saw the telescope. "That must have cost a mint."

"It was pretty expensive, but since Grandpa left me a pile of money and I've invested wisely," Jonathan explained, "I thought I'd indulge myself. Care to join us tonight for a little stargazing? Afterwards, I thought I'd conjure up the Battle of the Nile, for the pleasure and edification of all!"

Jonathan and Lewis hauled the telescope to the centre of the back yard, where they would have a reasonably good view of the heavens. Mrs Zimmermann stood beside Rose Rita, watching them wrestle the instrument into place. She folded her arms across her chest and shook her head. "If you're going to be serious about this astronomy, Frazzle Face, you're going to have to get that thing up higher, where trees won't block your view. Maybe you can knock a hole in the ceiling of Castle Barnavelt and put an observatory dome there!"

"Maybe," agreed Jonathan cheerfully. "Or maybe I'll buy the Hawaii House and take the roof off that sleeping porch on the top. That would be a place for a telescope."

Lewis wasn't really sure if his uncle was kidding or not. The Hawaii House stood a few streets away in New Zebedee. The man who had built it back in the 1800s had been a representative of the United States government to the Sandwich Islands, which was what the Hawaiian Islands were called back then. After spending years there, the man had retired to New Zebedee and had built a spectacular house in the style of a tropical mansion. Among its features was a sleeping veranda on the roof. In Hawaii the heat at night would have made that a comfortable bedroom, though in Michigan's climate it couldn't be used more than a few months a year. In fact, local people said that the original builder of the Hawaii House died one January night when he decided to sleep there and froze solid.

They played with the telescope for a while, with Uncle Jonathan showing Mrs Zimmermann how the electric motor worked and how the eyepieces slid into their little tube. He aimed the telescope at the top of a fairly distant tree and adjusted the spotting scope, which was a much smaller telescope attached to the main one. It was easy to aim, and when a target was lined up, the large telescope also showed the same thing. Lewis peered into the eyepiece, which made everything look sixty times closer than it was. Still, Lewis was amazed at how crisp and clear every leaf appeared. He also noticed that the tree looked upside down in the eyepiece.

"That's because this is an astronomical telescope," declared Uncle Jonathan. "It flips the image top to bottom, so when you look at the moon through it, north is at the bottom and south is at the top." He looked around. "Say, where is Rose Rita?"

"I don't know," said Lewis. "I'll go find her." He ran to the kitchen door and almost collided with her. "Where were you?" Lewis asked.

In a loud voice, Rose Rita said, "I had to visit the bathroom." Then, whispering to Lewis, she added, "I was really looking at the stuff Mrs Zimmermann brought over in the folder. Want to hear about it?"

Lewis turned and said, "Uncle Jonathan, we're gonna watch some TV."

His uncle waved at him. Lewis and Rose Rita went to the front parlour. Lewis switched on the TV, and when it warmed up, he found a Detroit Tigers baseball game. "That was kind of sneaky of you," he said to Rose Rita.

"I know," replied Rose Rita. "I'm not exactly proud of myself, but I thought it had to be done. Mrs Zimmermann's been looking up stuff about the Clabbernongs. Want to hear?"

Lewis said, "I guess I'd better."

"OK." Rose Rita began to hold up fingers as she counted off the items in the folder. "First, there's a photocopy of a newspaper article from the 1920s about the Clabbernong place. Some scientists thought the plants were infected by a fungus, but they couldn't track it down. The fellow who had bought the farm just moved away and abandoned it. Second, there's an obituary about Elihu Clabbernong from 1947. It just says he died of acute pneumonia and that he was eighty-four years old. Third, there's a piece of paper with 'Mephistopheles P. Moote, Attorney-at-Law' written on it, and an office address in Kalamazoo."

Lewis frowned. "Wasn't that the name of Elihu's lawyer?"

"You bet it was," said Rose Rita. "I think we ought to investigate him."

"Maybe we won't have to," argued Lewis. "Nothing's happened so far. Maybe we should leave the farm alone, and—"

"Your uncle doesn't think so," Rose Rita pointed out. "And neither do I."

"But why do we need to rock the boat?" asked Lewis, his tone woeful.

Rose Rita shook her head in a pitying way. "All right," she said. "If you're too scared to help me—"

"I didn't say that!" protested Lewis. He knew he had lost the argument already. "What do you think we ought to do?" he asked.

"Lots of things," answered Rose Rita. "See if this lawyer, Moote, knows anything. Figure out that peculiar paragraph from Elihu Clabbernong's will. Find out if anybody has made sense of Jebediah's crazy journal. Keep an eye out."

"All right," agreed Lewis. "But promise me that if we can't turn anything up by next week, we'll forget the whole thing. OK? I don't want this to be my life's work or anything."

"Bored already?" asked Rose Rita with a crooked smile. "Hey, Lewis, I'm just as scared as you are. But that doesn't mean we can leave our friends in the lurch."

"You can't be as scared as I am," grumbled Lewis. "I don't think that's possible."

All went well that evening, up to a point. Mrs Zimmermann dryly observed that her Saturday-evening dinners were getting to be a habit, but for all her pretend grumpiness she prepared a delicious meal: tender roast chicken, some incredibly sweet fresh corn on the cob, mounds of bright green peas dripping with butter sauce, and some wonderful home-baked rolls, with a piping hot apple pie and vanilla ice cream for dessert. Afterwards, Lewis and Rose Rita pitched in to help with the dishes, while Jonathan went out into the back yard and fiddled with the telescope as the sun sank and it became dark.

By the time Lewis, Rose Rita, and Mrs Zimmermann all trooped outside, a few stars were glittering overhead. The moon was a little more than half full, and Uncle Jonathan had aimed the telescope at it. "Lewis," he said, "want to take a peek at the surface of another world?"

Lewis squinted through the eyepiece at the image of the moon, glaring white in places, smooth and grey in others. The craters, especially near its ragged edge, were pools of jet black. The magnified face of the moon shimmered a little. Lewis found it absolutely enchanting.

Rose Rita took her turn next, then Mrs Zimmermann. "Very pretty," she said. "Any planets up there?"

"Sure," replied Jonathan. "Let me make a few

adjustments." He swung the telescope tube around, peered through the spotting scope, and then twiddled some knobs. "Take a look at this," he said.

Lewis again was first. He saw a pale yellow disk with a thin white ring around it. "Saturn!" he said.

"A-plus!" boomed Uncle Jonathan with a chuckle. "Don't hog the eyepiece, now!"

After they had all taken a look, Jonathan asked, "Any more special requests?"

In an innocent-sounding voice, Rose Rita asked, "Are there any comets we could look at?"

Lewis almost felt a chill in the air. Then Jonathan coughed and said, "There's supposed to be one. I'll have to line up the telescope with the setting circles, though. You can't see the comet yet with a small instrument like the spotting scope. Let me see." He fooled with the setting circles, looked in the eyepiece, and made more adjustments. Finally he said, "See what you think."

Lewis saw a fuzzy star with a bright red

centre. Then he realised that the blur around the star was really the coma, the part of a comet's tail that surrounds the icy head. With the aid of the telescope, Lewis could make out the tail itself, stretching away from the central red glare at an angle. "Does it have a name?" he asked.

"Not yet," said Uncle Jonathan. "It's got a number, though. If what the magazines say is correct, we'll be able to see it next week without a telescope. It's whizzing in pretty fast." After everyone else had looked at the comet, Uncle Jonathan said, "Let's call it a night. Tell you what: we'll have our special show on Monday. The Fourth of July deserves a few fireworks."

Lewis agreed, but only halfheartedly. His uncle clearly dreaded something.

And that only made Lewis feel more apprehensive than ever.

Monday night came, and Uncle Jonathan prepared to cast his illusion spell. He had cleared the telescope and the lawn furniture from the back yard. With Mrs Zimmermann, Lewis, and Rose Rita waiting in a line behind him, Uncle Jonathan stood almost in the middle of the yard. He lifted his walking stick and waved it mysteriously. Instantly a swirling fog condensed right out of the air. For a second Lewis couldn't see a thing. Then the mists billowed and faded, and salty spray drifted against Lewis's face. He and the others stood at the railing of an old-fashioned sailing ship. Lewis could feel the deck beneath his feet rising and falling as the craft cut through the water. Here and there lights gleamed from other vessels, but no gunfire sounded. The battle had not yet begun.

"We are aboard a ship in Nelson's squadron on the night of 1st August 1798," Jonathan said solemnly. "Our warship is a frigate that Nelson has sent into Aboukir Bay in the Mediterranean, near the mouth of the River Nile. We are slipping in to attack a French fleet, and I want you to keep an eye on the French ship of the line *L'Orient,* because just at midnight it's going to—"

Just what the ship was going to do Lewis did not find out. The deck lurched, tilted, and plunged, and they all staggered for balance. For a panic-stricken moment Lewis thought they had struck a rock.

Suddenly a lurid red light bathed everything. Looking up, Lewis saw that the glare streamed from the comet—but not as he had seen it in the telescope. It hung straight overhead, and its fiery heart blazed as bright as the foil moon, with its long tail streaming nearly halfway to the horizon.

"Jonathan—" began Mrs Zimmermann.

"I don't know what's wrong!" shouted Jonathan, waving his cane. Nothing happened. "Florence, I need your help!"

Lewis felt Rose Rita grab his arm. Their ship was *not* sailing in any bay. No other craft were about. A choppy, empty sea, the colour of blood in the light from the comet, stretched out in all directions. Something was rising from the water ahead of them, just off the port bow of the ship.

With a gasp, Lewis saw an enormous octopus

or squid break the surface of the water. Its tentacles writhed. Probably its normal colour was a sickly, mottled white, but in the light from the comet, it gleamed like fresh liver. Impossibly, the squirming beast rose even more, with blood-red streams pouring off it. Lewis heard himself shriek. He felt half crazed with terror.

The squid-thing wasn't an animal at all.

It was the horrible head of a gigantic human form!

And the monster, chest deep in the sea, was striding right towards them!

CHAPTER NINE

In a harsh voice Mrs Zimmermann chanted a magic spell. For a moment, jagged, purple lightning bolts flickered all around the ship. Then, like water flowing down a drain, the lightning streamed into the monster's body.

Lewis could not tear his gaze away from the weird scene. The giant seemed to swell, looking stronger than ever. "It's not working!" Lewis screamed.

At the same moment the creature screeched.

Lewis saw that the wriggling tentacles were like a hideous moustache, and beneath them the monstrosity's mouth gaped ten feet wide. Its teeth were like a shark's teeth, and its voice was a shrill, wavering roar.

"Hang on," yelled Mrs Zimmermann. "I can't fight it! My magic only makes it stronger! I'm going to try to counteract your spell, Jonathan. You know what it's like when you try to mix different kinds of magic—so hold on to Lewis and Rose Rita!"

Lewis felt his uncle's hand on his shoulder, and he gripped Jonathan's arm. He wanted to close his eyes, to shut out that terrible sight, but he was too afraid even to do that. The monstrous creature was reaching out for them with fish-scaled arms and grasping webbed claws. A nauseating reek of decaying fish washed over Lewis. He was only dimly aware of Mrs Zimmermann gesturing and waving her arms. Then he felt as if *he* had been struck by lightning. A shocking jolt took his breath away. A sickening sensation of plummeting, tumbling, and then—*oof!*—he fell hard to the ground. The *ground*. Not the deck of a ship!

Lewis lay face down in short-clipped grass. He could smell it. Its blades tickled his palms and his cheeks. He sensed his uncle kneeling next to him. Lewis raised his head, blinked, and saw that the unnatural bloody light had gone. Crickets chirped nearby. They were once more in the Barnavelts' back yard.

"Is—is everyone OK?" asked Lewis's uncle, his voice dazed and hoarse.

"I am," replied Rose Rita.

"I—I guess so," said Lewis at the same time.

Mrs Zimmermann stood unsteadily a few feet away. "Let's get inside," she said, her tone strained and low.

They all stumbled into the kitchen. Mrs Zimmermann's appearance shocked Lewis as she slumped into a chair. Her hair, never especially neat, was tangled in strands around her face. She had turned very pale, her skin almost waxy, and dark circles smudged the flesh beneath her eyes. Uncle Jonathan brought her a glass of water, which she drank gratefully. "Are you all right, Florence?" he asked, his voice anxious.

Heaving a sigh, she nodded. "I think so. I didn't have my umbrella, so half my power was unavailable to begin with. And that—that creature gobbled up most of the rest of it! If I'd tried to hit it with another spell, I think the effort might have killed me."

Rose Rita asked, "What was it? Where were we?"

Uncle Jonathan shook his head. "I have no earthly idea, Rose Rita. And for that matter, we may not have *been* on Earth! We may have been on some other planet—or in some other time. Something twisted my spell. It was supposed to be a simple illusion, and illusions can't hurt you. But that monster was real."

"Real—and very strange," put in Mrs Zimmermann. "It isn't merely immune to magic. It seems to absorb magic, to thrive on it. I've never heard of anything so outlandish."

"H-has anything like that ever happened

before?" asked Lewis. "I m-mean, your illusion spell going wrong, Uncle Jonathan?"

"Not to me," Jonathan said. "Mrs Zimmermann and I are going to have to figure this one out." With a frown, he added, "Hmm. Seems to me that we should start with the books by H. P. Lovecraft. They're supposed to be fiction, but if memory serves, he described just such creatures."

"I wish it *had* been fiction," Rose Rita muttered. "I guess the Battle of the Nile is off for good."

"Well," said Uncle Jonathan, "at least for the time being. Sorry for the disappointment, kids."

"It's OK," Lewis said. "Uh, maybe I should walk Rose Rita home."

"That would be a good idea," agreed Jonathan. "Everything seems back to normal, so you should be safe. In the meantime, Mrs Zimmermann and I will put our heads together about old Slimy. You two be careful."

Rose Rita gave him a sickly grin. "We will."

"I'm sorry," repeated Jonathan.

With a shrug, Rose Rita replied, "Well, you promised us fireworks!"

It really wasn't very far to Rose Rita's house—just a few minutes' walk. She and Lewis could hear the distant, muffled pops of skyrockets and firecrackers going off at the athletics field. That would be the New Zebedee Fourth of July show, sponsored by the chamber of commerce. To Lewis, the distant explosions sounded small and trivial. Especially compared to what he had seen.

"Thanks for walking me home," said Rose Rita. "That's brave of you."

Lewis felt a little embarrassed. "Uncle Jonathan and Mrs Zimmermann need to talk." He shivered and looked around. The moon was almost full, though its pale light served mainly to make shadows darker and more mysterious than ever. Lewis confessed, "I don't mind walking you to your front door. But to tell you the truth, I think I'll run all the way home!"

Rose Rita was hurrying as they turned on to Mansion Street beneath a yellow street lamp.

Above them, white moths whirled around the bulb, like tiny planets madly orbiting a star. Beneath the light, Rose Rita gave Lewis a glance. "You'd better come over tomorrow morning. We're going to have to do some investigating."

"I know," mumbled Lewis. It was not something he looked forward to doing, but he felt that he had to carry on. "I'll be over early."

They didn't say anything else. At her front door, Rose Rita said, "See you tomorrow," and then she hurried in.

Lewis began to walk back to High Street, but all around him the night seemed alive. He thought of evil beings lurking just beyond his sight. He remembered the ghastly stench of the monstrous creature. In his mind Lewis could picture the slimy, blood-red water dripping from its squirming tentacles.

He walked faster, then broke into a run. The street lamps made yellow islands of light on the face of a great darkness. Lewis ran from one to the next, as desperate as a swimmer trying to reach solid ground before drowning.

His breath came harsh in his throat as he pounded up the hill. All his attention was fixed on his own house, perched at the summit.

He did not notice the unfamiliar old black Buick parked just down the slope and across the street, at the edge of the Hanchett house's front yard.

Nor did he notice two pairs of eyes that glared at him with anger and hatred.

"Who's the brat?" growled Mephisto Moote. "I thought Barnavelt was a bachelor."

"How should I know who he is, you old fool?" snarled his wife. "I don't know a soul in this dreary town. We didn't move here to socialise, you know!"

"Shut up, shut up," grumbled the man. "Well, this is where the magic happened. I sensed it at once. It caused a dimensional rift. One of the Great Old Ones stirred when it happened. That's the influence of the Red Star. It will be visible to the naked eye next week, as the moon wanes."

Mrs Moote nodded her agreement. "Most of

the magic must have leaked into the other dimension. Still, some was bound to stay on this side. Maybe its power reached as far as the old bridge site. This could be just the thing to awaken our friend. I'll drive us to the place."

"Yes. Magic is just the thing to bring him to full consciousness. Hurry," urged her husband. "Hurry. I must see."

The woman let the old car roll silently down the hill until they were well past the Barnavelts' house. Then she started the engine, which caught with a loud bang. They drove through town and turned south. Within a few minutes, she pulled the car off the road near the new bridge across Wilder Creek.

Both of the old people climbed out of the car. Mephisto Moote leaned on his cane as he complained his way to the bank of the stream. Standing there, ten feet above the water, he took a deep sniff. "Ahh," he said. "I was right! He comes! He comes!"

The woman stood at his shoulder. Both of them stared down at the water. It was boiling with bubbles that shone faintly iridescent in the moonlight.

"It's too early," said the woman. "Your calculations said he would not rise until the full of the moon. That won't be until tomorrow night."

"Quiet!" rasped Moote. "Stupid woman, don't you realise that magic tips the balance? If our friend is strong enough, he will come now—look! Look at that!"

Something had risen in the water. It was roughly circular, a couple of feet across, pale grey and white and shot through with red and purple veins that throbbed as the two people stared down, fascinated. Whatever it was quivered like gelatin. It hardly seemed solid at all.

Then a line a foot long appeared in its surface. It split, and suddenly an enormous yellow-green eye was staring up at them. Another appeared, and weirdly, between them, a blubbery mouth opened.

In a thick voice, the creature in the water said, "I rise."

The eyes and mouth drifted horribly. More lumps and bubbles appeared in that bizarre flesh. An arm formed, but the hand on the end had ten writhing foot-long tentacles. The mass dragged itself to the shore and painfully pulled itself from the water.

Mephisto Moote dropped to his bony knees. "My Lord!" he said, his voice exultant. "You have returned to us!"

"W-weak," sighed the heaving mass of flesh. It throbbed and lurched aimlessly beside the stream a few feet beneath Moote's kneeling form.

"You'll be stronger," said Mrs Moote, putting her hand on her husband's shoulder. "We'll give you magic to eat!"

"An-n-nd?" groaned the freakish creature. "An-n-n-d?"

"And lives," said Moote quickly. "Many of them."

"Souls," cooed the woman. "You shall have souls to eat!"

For a second the terrible thing was quiet. Then it said, "I hunger! I hunger!" It surged, and suddenly it took on the rough shape of a human. A human twelve feet tall, with stumpy legs that ended in round pads like pancakes, and two arms that were more like the tentacles of an octopus.

And it began to climb up to the Mootes.

All the time, its features changed and slipped. One eye was now high on its forehead, four inches across and green. The other eye was much smaller, red, and where its right ear should have been. Its mouth gaped, a hole into unimaginable darkness.

"I hunger!" It reared as it towered above the Mootes, dripping and rippling in the moonlight. "I hunger!"

And at the sound, everything else in the night fell silent.

CHAPTER TEN

On Wednesday night, the Capharnaum County Magicians Society met again at the Barnavelt house. This time, though, Lewis and Rose Rita had no opportunity to eavesdrop. Before they had a chance to hide in the secret passage, Mrs Zimmermann took one group of magicians into the kitchen to tell them about the eerie creature that her magic had been unable to stop. The others were in the study, giving their reports to Uncle Jonathan.

With both ends of the secret passage closed

to them, Lewis and Rose Rita held their own council of war in the back yard. "Did you read the paper today?" asked Rose Rita.

"Not yet," said Lewis. "Why?"

"There's a story on page two about something that seems very familiar," replied Rose Rita in a grim tone. "At some time during Monday night, a strip of grass along one side of Wilder Creek Road died and turned grey."

Lewis looked at her. They were sitting in lawn chairs, and though the evening was getting dark, a spill of warm yellow light from the kitchen windows illuminated Rose Rita's face. "Like the Clabbernong farm," whispered Lewis.

"Just like that," agreed Rose Rita. "The county agent says it's probably a fungus, but we know better. And there's something even worse. The track is leading towards town."

Lewis clamped his teeth tight to keep them from chattering. It was a warm, clear evening. Night insects trilled all around them. Everything seemed normal and safe. Lewis tried to force himself to relax. "I wonder what caused that."

"Whatever it was that—oh, my gosh!" Rose Rita was leaning back in her lawn chair, staring straight up.

Lewis followed her gaze. His skin felt as if ants were crawling on it. Staring up into the sky, he could see the Red Star comet. It was much dimmer than in the telescope, with just a whisk of a tail, but Lewis could see it clearly. "Time's running out," he said.

"It sure is," replied Rose Rita. "Look, do you remember what your uncle said about the writer H. P. Lovecraft? Well, I checked a couple of his books out of the library. I don't know where he got his stuff, but he talks about Great Old Ones and unseen horrors and all sorts of strange things. And guess what? When I was signing my name on the library card, I noticed who had checked those books out just before me."

"Who?" Lewis asked, not sure he even wanted to know.

"A certain Mrs E. Moote," said Rose Rita. "And I found out where she lives. On Field

158

Street. That's just outside of town to the south, a street that forks off from Wilder Creek Road."

"She must be tied into all this somehow," said Lewis. "But what can we do?"

Rose Rita sighed. "I just don't know. Look, let's go in. That red comet can't be healthy for us. Maybe it's got atomic rays coming out of it."

"I don't think comets have any kind of rays coming out of them," said Lewis. "They don't shine by themselves. They reflect sunlight."

Rose Rita sniffed. "I don't care. This one's bad for *my* health. I don't feel well at all."

Lewis started to get up, and as he did, he had the strangest sensation. It was as if a light popped on in his brain, then went out again, like a flashbulb. "What did that paragraph in Elihu's will say?" he asked slowly.

"I've memorised it," Rose Rita told him. "It says, and I quote, 'Meanings may have other meanings. One thing I have learned is that the heart is the seat of the soul. The soul is the life.

And the key to finding the life is, at the very bottom, a healthy heart.' If you ask me, old Elihu seemed a bit crazy."

Desperately, Lewis closed his eyes. He felt so close—he almost had it—but then . . . the vague notion had fled.

"I thought I could make sense of it," he said. "Meanings and other meanings. Double meanings?"

"What is it?" asked Rose Rita.

Lewis shook his head. "I don't know. I'm not sure now."

"Maybe it'll come back to you," said Rose Rita. "Tomorrow I want to go spy out the Moote house. Maybe the key is there."

"Let's not take chances," pleaded Lewis.

"No fear of that," promised Rose Rita. "We're going to be very careful."

Thursday morning was cloudy, with a threat of thunder hanging in the air, but the storm did not break loose. At nine o'clock, Lewis and Rose Rita rode their bikes out of town again.

This trip was not a very long one—only a mile from the centre of town. A narrow street led off to the right. It didn't have a street sign, but Rose Rita said that on the map it was called Field Street.

The houses were all small and widely spaced—wood-frame buildings, cottages, and bungalows. Lewis thought they seemed like the sort of homes that retired people lived in. Most of them had vegetable gardens in the back yards. But one yard was choked with lush green weeds except for a dozen scattered grey patches, which looked just like the plants on the Clabbernong farm. Rose Rita didn't even have to tell Lewis that this was the Moote house. An old black Buick was parked near a big cedar tree in the front yard. Rose Rita rode past the house, then turned down a grassy lane that led towards a narrow brook. The weeds on either side had grown taller than Lewis.

When they reached the stream, they stopped. "Now what?" asked Lewis.

"Now we watch," said Rose Rita, carefully

parting the weeds. From here they could see the house. "In fact, I'll bet we can sneak up on them."

"I don't think that's a good idea," objected Lewis, but Rose Rita was already creeping forwards, bent double. She moved carefully, disturbing the weeds as little as possible. Lewis followed, hoping no snakes were crawling through this tangle. Closer and closer they edged, until they were within a few feet of an open window. Lewis could hear two quarrelling voices: a crabby old man and a woman who spoke in a hoarse, husky tone.

The woman was saying, "Of course he doesn't remember being Jebediah Clabbernong, you fool. There's too much of the Other in that body. And his cursed nephew kept him prisoner with that terrible iron bridge for all those years."

"I don't want to change if I can't remember anything," complained the old man. "What good is that? It would be like dying, and I don't want to die!"

"You will remember," said the woman. "Because your body will not be cremated before you change! It won't be pinned to the bottom of a stream for years and years, while the alien flesh absorbs every particle of your brain! You'll still be Mephistopheles Moote—you'll just have a new body, a new flesh, like our friend!"

Lewis leaned close to Rose Rita and whispered, "What are they talking about?"

Rose Rita shook her head. She didn't know.

"Aahh!" snarled the man. "I've half a mind not to go through with this!"

"What!" shrieked the woman. "Back out now, when the Red Star is in the night sky?"

Lewis and Rose Rita exchanged a glance. *We've got to tell*, Lewis mouthed silently.

Rose Rita frowned and shrugged. *Maybe*, the gesture said.

The woman was yelling now. "Are you mad? All we have to do is trick those foolish friends of the Barnavelt man into attacking our little pet with magic—the stronger, the better! The idiots won't know that any magical attack will make him more and more powerful, until he can open the gateway for the other Great Old Ones!"

"And they will come from the star," said the old man. "Yes, yes, Ermine, I know all that! Well, when should we attack them?"

"Soon!" replied the woman. "As soon as possible! There's a weakness, you know. Jebediah Clabbernong thought he was being so clever, holding back a part of himself! Elihu hid that part so well, we can't find it. I'm sure Jebediah's precious nephew didn't destroy it—he would know enough to realise that it could only be dealt with when the Red Star shone. But that's the weak point! That's human enough so that magic might work against it."

Lewis felt Rose Rita squeeze his arm. He was leaning forwards, conscious of everything—the tickle of weeds on his cheek, the oppressive weight of the sultry, cloudy day, the harsh voice of the woman. His head was spinning. What weakness was she talking about?

"What do you want to do?" asked the man. "Go back out to that blasted farm and comb every inch of ground again? The animals that died there in 1885 are stirring again, you know.

That's the work of the star. Ugh! The stench of them!"

"No, no, no!" shouted the woman. "I've given up on finding that little prize package. Curse Jebediah and his spell for separating the soul from the body! No, what we have to do is make sure that what *we've* hidden stays hidden. It must emerge only in the light of the star. I think we should check."

"I'm not driving to the waterworks every five minutes!" barked the man. "If you want to go and look, go! I have to rest!"

"Oh, no, you don't," said the woman. "I'm going to keep my eye on you. We're not parting from each other until we both change. I know you! You're selfish enough to change without me!"

The old man must have left the room, because his voice faded to a whining, angry mutter. A moment later a door slammed, and all was silent. Rose Rita squirmed around, and Lewis followed her to their bikes.

"Come on," she said.

"Where?" asked Lewis. "Shouldn't we go back and tell—"

"Not yet," interrupted Rose Rita. "Those two have hidden something. We've got to check that out."

"You mean the waterworks," said Lewis.

"Come on," said Rose Rita again, and she climbed on to her bike. Lewis got on his too, and they pedalled back to town and over to Spruce Street. At the bottom of a hill were four or five vacant lots, and the city waterworks, a big brick building that hummed with machinery. Behind the waterworks was the reservoir, a round, clear pond protected by a high chain-link fence. Across the street was a green park, through which Spruce Creek meandered. A few families were there, tossing baseballs and having picnics.

"I don't see anything," said Lewis. "I think we'd better go and—"

Rose Rita hopped off her bike and stared downwards. "Look at this."

She was pointing to the ground. Feeling his

stomach heave, Lewis saw streaks in the grass. Streaks of grey, brittle decay. "The grass is dying," he said.

"The trail leads towards the bridge," said Rose Rita. "Come on."

The brick footbridge crossed a deep part of the stream and was built over three big barrel arches. As Lewis and Rose Rita rolled their bikes across, a sickening odour made Lewis gag. "What's that?"

Rose Rita leaned over the bridge. "I think it's coming from underneath. Ugh! It smells as if something's crawled in there and died!"

The two friends looked at each other. Lewis could tell they both had the same thought. "Do we have to?" he asked.

Rose Rita grimaced. "I think we do."

They left their bikes, crossed the bridge, and clambered down the bank. The brick arches were so tall that they could both stand under the first one. Here the creek was about a dozen feet across. Lewis and Rose Rita stood on the bank beside the first arch and looked at the water under the middle arch. It had the dark, greenish colour of deeper water, and now and then a few scummy yellow bubbles came up from the depths. It looked as if a rock or something was a foot under the surface.

"Wait a minute," said Rose Rita. She scrambled around the stream bank until she found a fallen tree branch, thin but long and springy. She brought it back. "Let's see if we can reach it."

Standing at the very edge of the water, Rose Rita leaned forwards and prodded with the stick. It was just a little too short. "Let's go," said Lewis.

"Not yet," muttered Rose Rita. "Hold my hand. Lean back. And don't let go!"

Lewis gripped her left wrist. Rose Rita bent far out over the water and tried again. This time the stick touched something. "It feels spongy," reported Rose Rita. "It feels like—"

She pitched forwards so hard that Lewis thought they were both going into the water. He tugged back, just as she let go of the stick, they toppled on to the bank. Lewis saw the tree branch thrash wildly. A writhing tentacle had wrapped around it. It tossed the stick aside and slipped under the surface. Then something round and nasty-looking broke the surface of the water. It was lumpy, grey, and veined with red and blue.

And it opened a ghastly dead-looking eye to stare at them!

CHAPTER ELEVEN

The face—if it *was* a face—sank immediately in a swirl of water. Lewis and Rose Rita leaped to their feet and stumbled up the bank of the creek. At the top they turned fearfully, but nothing showed that the hideous, quivering thing had even been there. The smooth green water flowed on without a ripple or a bubble.

Still—the creature had to be down there. It might return.

"Let's go," said Lewis, climbing on to his bike. Just as he did, the thunder that had been building all morning resounded with an earth-shaking rumble. The wind gusted. As Lewis pedalled across the bridge, he saw that everyone had deserted the park in the few minutes he and Rose Rita had been near the stream. The tops of the spruce and fir trees whipped back and forth, and above them, the ragged clouds swirled past like dark smoke. A white bolt of lightning split the sky overhead.

Lewis looked over his shoulder and saw that Rose Rita was close behind him. She was leaning over the handlebars, her face pale. Her eyes opened wide. "Look out!" she yelled.

Lewis jerked his head around. He was almost at the street. The battered old black Buick rolled to the kerb, right in front of him. Lewis put on the coaster brake of his bike, but on the grass the rear tyre just skidded. The car loomed closer! Desperately, Lewis swerved, lost his balance, and tumbled from his bike. At first, everything seemed to happen in nightmarish slow motion.

He saw the grass coming towards his face, each green blade seeming distinct and sharp.

With a sickening thud, his head hit the ground, and the world exploded in yellow light. Lewis had a vague sensation of turning a somersault, then he slammed flat on his back against the concrete pavement so hard that he lost his breath. His lungs pumped, but no air came in. Everything faded out. For a second he wondered if he were dying.

At last his breath came back with a great shuddering wheeze. He heard a clatter off to one side, and Rose Rita was kneeling over him, pleading, "Are you OK?"

That's a silly question, he thought, but he didn't have breath enough to talk. And the pain had started, the sharp hot sting of cuts on his knees and the palm of one hand, the throb of a lump high on his forehead.

Two other people leaned over him. To Lewis, they seemed to waver in and out of focus. His uncle and Mrs Zimmermann? No, an old man and an old woman. But not until he heard the woman's low-pitched, husky voice did Lewis realise that they were the Mootes. "My goodness, young man, you took quite a tumble!"

Lewis's skin crawled at the sound. If he could have gathered the strength, he would have sprung up and run for his life. But all he could do was lie there, fighting for air.

The old man stood leaning on a cane, while the woman knelt next to Rose Rita. Mr Moote said, "Perhaps we should take you to our home. We could call—"

"*No!*" said Lewis. He still had hardly any breath, but he would have to have been dead not to object. He said, "Uh, no, thanks. I—I'm fine. Just had the wind knocked out of me." His voice sounded weak, uncertain, and on the verge of tears.

"Are you sure, dear?" asked the woman, smoothing his hair away from his forehead.

Lewis was terrified. He half expected her touch to be as cold as a snake's. He did not know how badly he was hurt—he was scraped

up and bruised, at the very least—but he fought hard not to cry. "I'm fine!" He tried to force his voice to be calm. "I've had lots worse falls than this, really. My sister Nancy will tell you."

"Uh, sure," said Rose Rita. She blinked behind her round glasses. Of the two, Rose Rita was always the quickest to dream up some improbable story. Now she said, "Uh, see, Billy went to the circus with Mum and Dad when he was four, and they had this big grizzly bear that rode a bike. The bear could do wheelies, and he could ride with no hands, and he rode across a tightrope. Well, ever since we saw all that, Billy's been trying to do the stunts that bear did—"

"Come on," Lewis said, getting up and going to his bike. His steps felt wobbly, as if the earth were quivering like jelly under his feet. "Mum and Dad will be mad if we get wet, and it's gonna pour with rain in a minute." Painfully, he lifted his bike, which did not seem to be seriously damaged. He climbed aboard, said, "Thanks!" and pushed off. Now he could tell that both his knees and the palm of his left hand were badly skinned. His fall had ripped two big holes in his jeans legs, and he could feel a warm trickle of blood down his shins. But he wouldn't have stayed near Mephistopheles and Ermine Moote for a thousand dollars.

Rose Rita came pedalling up next to him. "Hey, are you all right? That was a bad fall."

"I think I'm OK," said Lewis, panting. The pain was making tears well out of both his eyes. He felt them cool on his cheeks as the wind blew in his face. "We have to tell Uncle Jonathan about this."

"How about writing another note?" asked Rose Rita. "You go tell your uncle that you fell off your bike. Don't let him know how it happened. Just say it was an accident. I'll bet you anything he takes you to the doctor. While he does, I'll go home and get the pad and write the letter. I'll tell him not to use any magic, and I'll tell him that the Mootes are somehow behind all this."

"OK," replied Lewis, whose head was pounding. He had a lump on the front of his skull, in the hair above his left eyebrow. At least he wasn't seeing double. But he did feel nauseated, and he was glad when at last they reached 100 High Street.

Rose Rita ran inside and emerged a moment later with Uncle Jonathan in tow. Lewis had just stood his bike up when Jonathan hurried over and took one look at him. "Into the car, Lewis. I think we'd better go visit Dr Humphries. Thanks, Rose Rita. You'd better get home. This storm's going to cut loose any second."

Jonathan and Lewis drove over to Dr Humphries's clinic, and just as they walked in, the rain began to pour. The nurse at the front desk took Lewis straight back to an examining room, with Uncle Jonathan at his heels. A moment later the doctor came in, his expression concerned.

Lewis liked Dr Humphries, a big, comfortable-looking man with a voice like a bass viol. The doctor had him sit on the green examining table and took a look first at the bump on his head. "Hmm," he said. "Must've been quite a crack.

I'll wager that put a dent in the road! I'm going to shine a light in your eyes, Lewis. It's going to bother you a little but keep your eyes open. Look straight ahead." The penlight he held stabbed Lewis's eyes, making them water, but he didn't complain. Then Dr Humphries held up two fingers and asked Lewis how many he saw. Finally, Dr Humphries laughed. "They must grow 'em hardheaded in Wisconsin," he rumbled. "No concussion, which is the best news you've heard since Christmas. Now let's look at those scrapes and abrasions."

A few minutes later, patched up and bandaged, Lewis left the clinic with his uncle. The rain had settled in to a steady, dreary downpour, and as they drove through it, Uncle Jonathan said, "How on earth did you fall?"

Lewis said, "We were hurrying home because we heard thunder. I looked over my shoulder to see where Rose Rita was, and I almost hit a car. I swerved in time to miss it, but I fell off."

"Lewis, you have to be more careful," said Jonathan, shaking his head.

Though Lewis had been right on the edge of blurting out everything, that made him bite his tongue. What if his uncle became even more disappointed in him? And what would he say if he learned Lewis and Rose Rita had been snooping around, poking their noses into things that they should have left alone?

As soon as they had hurried into the house, Uncle Jonathan saw Rose Rita's new message. She had folded it and dropped it through the letterbox. It was on the same kind of yellow paper as the first note, written in the same blocky letters. Lewis was close enough to read what it said:

DEAR MR BARNAVELT,
YOU MUST NOT USE MAGIC AGAINST THE THREAT. MR AND MRS MOOTE KNOW MORE THAN THEY LET ON. SOMETHING HORRIBLE CAME FROM THE CLABBER-NONG FARM. IT IS NOW IN SPRUCE PARK, UNDER THE ARCHED BRIDGE. TAKE CARE!
    SIGNED, A FRIEND

Uncle Jonathan quickly folded the letter, said, "Hrmpf!" and then turned to Lewis. "How are you feeling?"

"Not so hot," Lewis confessed. "I've got an awful headache."

Jonathan felt his forehead. "No fever. Take a couple of aspirin for the pain. I think you'd better go to your room for a little while. You've been pretty badly banged up, and you're going to be sore as a boil tomorrow. Want an ice bag for your head?"

"No, I'll be all right," said Lewis.

Jonathan raised his eyebrows. "Sure? All right, then, go lie down for a while, until your head feels better. Meanwhile, I need to make some phone calls."

Lewis did not protest. He went to his bedroom and changed from his torn jeans into pyjamas. Then, instead of lying down, he put a pillow on the floor and knelt on it looking out the window. The day was dark, though the time was only a quarter to one. Sheets and sheets of pewter-coloured rain whipped down High Street. The trees lost twigs and leaves to the blustery wind. All down the hill, yellow lights shone in the windows of the houses. For some reason, they made Lewis feel lonely. He imagined himself as a homeless orphan, staring at the warm, safe houses of more fortunate kids.

Lewis wondered where Rose Rita was, and what she was up to. She was a good friend, but she could be so exasperating sometimes. Still, Lewis knew, Rose Rita was pretty sensible. She wasn't the kind of person who would take chances for no reason at all. Then Lewis thought about Mr and Mrs Moote, who acted so concerned when he had fallen. Mrs Moote had wanted him to go to their house. Lewis felt cold just thinking of that. If he had, would he ever have gotten out alive? What was the hideous thing in the water, and what did the Mootes have to do with it? Lewis had the queasy feeling that he had not seen the last of them—or of their "pet," the horrible creature in the water.

Watching the steady rain, Lewis let his mind

drift. His scrapes, bruises, and bumps ached. In a funny way the pressure of the pillow on his skinned knees helped. At least he didn't feel the ache as much. Lewis idly wondered how long it would take them to heal. "Heal," he murmured dreamily. He said the word over and over until it seemed to lose its meaning. Then he started on words that meant the same thing. "Health. Healthy. Well." When he said that, it was as if something suddenly clicked in his brain. It was almost like a jolt of electricity. The same thing had happened once before, but this time the light in his mind did not go off. Lewis jumped from a kneeling position straight to his bare feet. He forgot all about his throbbing headache and his bandaged knees. His eyes were wide. "Oh, my gosh!" he shouted.

Because this time he knew he was right. Meanings could have other meanings. Words that meant almost the same thing as each other could also mean different things—if you looked at them the right way, that is.

And Lewis had just done that. He felt his heart racing. Yes, he was sure.

Lewis had solved the riddle that Elihu Clabbernong had left in his will.

CHAPTER TWELVE

Lewis scrambled to get dressed, then rushed downstairs, yelling, "Uncle Jonathan!" He knew before he even got to the bottom of the stairs that Jonathan wasn't down there. The house had that funny echoing sound that houses get when nobody else is around. Jonathan's black cane with the crystal knob was gone from the blue willow-ware vase beside the front door. The cane was his magic wand, and if it was missing, then Jonathan had taken it for some purpose. Searching through the house, Lewis found a note on the kitchen table:

Hi Lewis,

Mrs Zimmermann and I have to run a couple of errands and check a few things out. If I'm not back until late, don't worry. I'll explain later. There's some roast beef in the refrigerator that you can heat up for dinner with a can of vegetable soup.

I hope your head is feeling better. If something very important had not come up, I'd never leave you alone like this. You can call Dr Humphries if you're feeling worse. His office and home telephone numbers are written on the inside back cover of the phone book. I hope to be back before midnight!

Love, Uncle J

A glance next door told Lewis that Mrs Zimmermann wasn't at home—her house was dark, though her car, the green Plymouth Cranbrook she called Bessie, was still in the driveway. Frantically, Lewis ran to the phone and dialled Rose Rita's number. Mrs Pottinger answered and called her daughter to the phone. Lewis almost hopped from one foot to another while he was waiting. A minute later he heard Rose Rita say, "Hello?"

"I got it!" said Lewis, all in a rush. "I figured it out!"

Rose Rita was quick on the uptake. "You solved Old Clabberhead's riddle? I'll be right over!"

Lewis could hear Mrs Pottinger object to that. Rose Rita must have put her hand over the receiver, because a muffled, quick argument followed. Finally, Rose Rita was back on the line: "I can't come over until after dinner, and then only if the rain lets up."

"Listen," said Lewis, "what did the Mootes say about Jebediah's spell for separating the soul?"

"They . . . didn't seem to like it," replied Rose Rita.

She paused, and Lewis guessed her mother was standing nearby. Cautiously, Rose Rita added, "That's all I know." Lewis heard Rose

Rita's mother call her, and Rose Rita said hastily, "I'll either come over or call you later. Don't do anything without me!"

As he hung up the phone, Lewis wondered what in the world he would do even *with* Rose Rita. If he was right—and he was sure he must be—someone else was going to have to help. Getting what Elihu had hidden all those years ago would not be a job for two kids. It would require—well, wizards and witches, probably. Someone a lot braver than he was, anyway.

All that afternoon, Lewis was jumpy and restless. Sometimes he paced. Sometimes he tried to watch television. He couldn't settle down, and every five minutes he looked at the clock as the hours crawled by.

At a little past five that afternoon, Lewis went to the French doors in the study and looked out into the yard. The rain was passing, with a few breaks in the clouds here and there. The sun was getting low, and where the grey clouds parted, Lewis could see blue sky and heaps of orange-red clouds. The colour reminded him of the comet, and that reminded him of the weird, pulsating creature he and Rose Rita had glimpsed—glimpsed? Poked with a stick!

Shivering, he turned away from the French doors and began to look through the books in the study. His uncle had floor-to-ceiling shelves of old volumes on many different subjects. One particular corner held books on magic.

Lewis looked through these until he found what he was looking for, van Schull's *Encyclopaedic Dictionary of Magic and the Magical Arts*. It was a huge, heavy old book, the size and weight of an unabridged dictionary. The binding was some dark leather with a pattern of diamond-shaped scales—but if the skin had come from a snake, it must have been an enormous one. Lewis lugged the tome over to the desk and dropped it with a thump. He turned on the green-shaded lamp and opened the volume. Like all old books, it had its own peculiar smell, dusty and dry but with a spicy undertone that tickled his nose.

Lewis turned the creamy, liver-spotted pages

carefully. Under "soul," he found a number of articles, but only one looked like what he was hunting for: "Soul, Separable."

Lewis bent close to the book to read the fine print:

Soul, Separable. Magicians in many lands have worked on spells to become invulnerable to harm and death by separating their souls from their living bodies. Once the spell is accomplished, the magician's soul may be hidden away, perhaps in a tree, a stone, a well, or a jewel; or it may be placed in an unusual part of the magician's body, so that he or she may continue to live even if the heart is pierced (see the stories of Achilles and his heel, Nisus and his royal hair, etc, under Souls, Oddly Placed).

More commonly, the soul is concealed in an unusual vessel, such as a flower, a stone, or a ruby. This vessel is hidden in a safe place, and until it is found and destroyed, releasing the captured spirit, the owner of the soul cannot truly die. Even if the magician's body is destroyed, it will slowly regenerate, as long as the soul is intact.

An old Norse tale, The Heartless Giant, *speaks of a sorcerous giant who hid his heart, which contained his soul, in an egg that was inside a duck that swam inside a hidden well that lay under a forgotten church located on a secret island in the centre of an unknown lake. In order to slay the giant, the hero of the story had not only to break the egg but first had to go on a long, dangerous quest to locate it. In the Irish story of Cano, Cano's soul was locked inside a stone, and until the stone was broken, Cano could not die.*

The spells for separating the soul from the body are infallibly evil ones and as such are unknown to good magicians. The Thaumaturgy *of Livius the Younger records only the first line of an incantation . . .*

There was more, but it told Lewis very little that was useful. He was more convinced than ever, though, that his guess had been right. He wished he knew where Uncle Jonathan and Mrs Zimmermann had gone.

Time seemed to crawl by. Lewis made a sandwich from the cold roast beef, but he ate it with little appetite. His injured knees felt stiff. At least the lump on his head was shrinking, though he had a spectacularly black left eye. He tossed nearly half of his sandwich in the garbage and paced the floor restlessly. The old house grew darker as the rain passed and the sun sank, and Lewis became more and more nervous. Every slap of a wet tree branch on a window made him jump. Each creak and groan of a floorboard under his feet startled him. He kept walking to the front door, opening it, and peering out into the street to see whether Rose Rita had arrived.

On one of these trips, he noticed something odd. To the right of the front door was a coatrack with a mirror in it. For as long as Lewis had lived in the house, the mirror had been magical, sometimes showing his face but more often scenes from strange, distant lands. Now light was flashing out of it, angular spears of crimson that danced and shimmered on the opposite wall. Lewis swallowed hard and looked into the glass.

It showed the comet, red as blood, against a dark night sky. The image rippled as if Lewis were peering at it through water. Sometimes it faded to a dull rusty colour, and sometimes it blazed to a red so bright that it hurt to look at it. Lewis threw his hand up to shield his vision, and then he saw, just above the comet, two staring eyes—human eyes. They shifted rapidly, as if their owner were looking for someone. Suddenly, they locked on to Lewis.

Lewis could see the shrivelled, grim face of Mephistopheles Moote. It hung there in the mirror, staring out balefully. The thin, wrinkled lips twitched into a sneer. Words flowed into Lewis's head, not spoken, but coming like a thought: "Well, well—'Billy', the boy who was hurt! The snoop!"

Lewis could not tear his gaze away.

The voice in his head said, "How is your 'sister,' Lewis Barnavelt? Is her name really Pottinger? Do you think she and her wretched family are safe from my anger? And does your foolish uncle know that he has only until midnight to live? The Earth will be swept clean of puny humans—and only I will live on forever in another form! The Great Old Ones shall claim dominion again! The triumph of the Red Star will be complete!"

Lewis thought he would lose his mind. An impression of high-pitched, hateful laughter filled his skull. He felt frozen. Then a sound, a real sound, jarred him: the harsh metallic jangle of the old mechanical doorbell to his left. He jerked his eyes towards the door, and in that instant the mirror went dark. The only vestige left was the angry howl of Mephistopheles Moote, fading like a mosquito's hum in Lewis's brain.

Lewis threw himself at the door and wrenched it open. Rose Rita stood there, her hand still out to turn the key of the doorbell again. "Lewis! What happened? You look awful!"

Lewis dragged her into the study, away from the mirror, and blurted out everything that had happened. "Midnight!" she said when he had finished. "It's already nearly six!"

"That's not all," Lewis told her.

"I know," she said. "You think you've solved the riddle in Elihu Clabbernong's will."

"I don't just think so—I know so!" said Lewis urgently.

"Spill it!" exclaimed Rose Rita.

Lewis's words tumbled out as he explained what a "separable soul" was. Then he said, "So here's what must have happened. Old Jebediah Clabbernong used a magic spell to take his soul out of his body and put it into something. Elihu knew that his uncle wasn't really dead when he had his body cremated. Somehow he found whatever it was that held Jebediah's soul. For some reason he couldn't destroy it—"

"Why not?" asked Rose Rita.

Lewis gave her an irritated glance. "How should I know? Maybe because it would let that monster we saw break loose! Or maybe it

196

was for some other magical reason. I don't know! But instead of destroying the thing that holds Jebediah's soul, Elihu hid it away. And I know where he put it!"

Rose Rita scowled at him. "Don't keep me on pins and needles, Lewis! Where?"

Triumphantly, Lewis quoted the will: "'The key to finding the life is, at the very bottom, a healthy heart.'" When Rose Rita just stared blankly at him, he added, "Meanings have other meanings, remember? Like 'life' could mean 'soul.' And if you're healthy, you're—?"

Rose Rita shrugged. "In good shape?"

Lewis shook his head impatiently. "Try again!"

Rolling her eyes, Rose Rita said, "You're strong. You're doing fine. You're well."

"Bingo!" said Lewis. "The key to finding the life—that would be old Jebediah's soul—is at the bottom, a well heart. *Well*, Rose Rita."

Behind her round glasses, Rose Rita's eyes widened. "Well! Old Creepy's soul is hidden in something that's in the well at the Clabbernong place!"

Lewis nodded. "And we have to get it out," he said.

For a moment the two friends stared at each other. Lewis didn't know about Rose Rita, but the very thought of returning to that horrible place made him feel sick.

But somehow, they had to do it.

Otherwise, they—and the rest of the world— had barely six hours to live.

CHAPTER THIRTEEN

"We'll never get out there and back on our bikes in time," wailed Rose Rita. "What can we do?"

"We have to try!" declared Lewis. He dashed down into the cellar and returned with a coil of rope and a long, heavy chrome-plated torch. He handed these to Rose Rita and ran up to his room for one final thing. Hurrying downstairs again, Lewis yelled, "Come on!"

They started out the back way, and Rose Rita cried, "Look! Mrs Zimmermann is at home!"

Sure enough, the side parlour window of Mrs Zimmermann's house was yellow with light. Lewis and Rose Rita ran over and pounded on the door.

To Lewis's surprise, a kindly woman opened it. "Lewis!" she said. "Rose Rita!"

"Mrs Jaeger!" Rose Rita blurted out. "What are you doing here?"

Mrs Mildred Jaeger gave her a sad kind of smile. "Well, dear, you know my magic isn't the most reliable. All the other magicians are gathering for something big tonight. Mrs Zimmermann forgot an amulet she may need, and, well, I was the one they could most easily spare, so I volunteered." She held up a small white box. "I hope it's what Mrs Zimmermann needs."

"*We* can help, Mrs Jaeger," said Lewis. "But you'll have to drive us out into the country."

"What happened to your poor eye?" asked Mrs Jaeger.

"I had a bump on the head, but it's not bad," Lewis told her. "Mrs Jaeger, you'll have to help us out." When she looked hesitant, he added,

"It's very important! We know all about the red comet and the Mootes."

"Oh, dear," said Mrs Jaeger. "Then I suppose I'd better drive you! My car's at the kerb."

The three of them piled into Mrs Jaeger's Chevrolet, and Rose Rita breathlessly gave her directions. By that time the last few clouds were breaking up over in the south. The sun was moving to the west. Lewis hoped that they could reach the Clabbernong place before it set. He didn't want to be there after dark.

Mrs Jaeger was a very careful driver, and even when she was speeding to the rescue, she puttered along at about forty miles per hour. They drove across the new bridge, made the turn at the little crossroads store, and reached the blighted Clabbernong farm just before seven. The sun was a bloated red disk, low in the sky. As they climbed out of the car, Lewis's head spun. It was not just the knock he had received earlier, but also the stench of the place.

They trooped behind the house, past the caved-in storm cellar—Rose Rita gave it a very wide berth—and came to the brick well. Only then did Lewis fully realise what he had to do. Someone had to be lowered into the dark pit. He couldn't ask Mrs Jaeger to go. And Rose Rita was deathly afraid of dark, closed places.

He had to do it.

He stood with his hands grasping the bricks at the rim of the well. Rising up on tiptoe, he stared down into the darkness. The well shaft was about five feet in diameter. Shining the torch down, Lewis could see moss-covered bricks, and perhaps twenty feet down, the reflection of his light on the face of the dark water. Rose Rita touched his shoulder. "Can you do it?" she asked in a shaky voice.

"I'll have to," replied Lewis, though he dreaded the thought of descending into the shaft. They tested the iron framework that held the windlass and bucket and found them strong, so Lewis tied one end of the rope to that. He looped the other end around his waist. Rose Rita unlaced one of her sneakers and threaded the lace through the ring at the base of the torch. She hung the torch around Lewis's neck. It felt heavy. "If I get in trouble down there, can you get me back up again?" he asked Rose Rita and Mrs Jaeger.

"We'll manage somehow," said Rose Rita with a sickly smile. "Be careful!"

Lewis coiled the rope and then climbed over the edge of the well. He tried to brace his feet on the mossy bricks, but they were very slippery. The rope burned his hands as he let himself down inch by inch. The hanging torch showed him just enough of the well shaft to see that nothing otherworldly or monstrous clung to the bricks. Otherwise, it wasn't much help.

After what seemed like hours, Lewis reached the end of the rope. Dangling there and holding on to the line with his left hand, he shone the light downwards. His toes swung about a yard above the water. It was still as a mirror, black as pitch. He could not tell if it was only a few inches deep or if it went down to an unknown abyss. Twisting on the rope, Lewis looked all the way around the shaft. Nothing. And then—

From the edges of what looked like a loose brick below him, he saw a faint glimmer of red light. Steadying himself, Lewis peered down. The brick must have been pried from the wall of the shaft, then replaced. It stuck out about an inch or so. The red glow leaked out all around it.

But it was maddeningly out of reach.

Grunting with effort, Lewis let go of the torch, letting it hang, and tugged at the knots. If he could lower himself another two feet, he might be able to—

The knots gave way suddenly! Lewis's injured left hand supported all his weight—and then the rope began to slip through it! Lewis made a desperate grab, missed, and plunged into cold water, shouting in alarm.

The frigid water came to Lewis's knees. He stood on slippery mud. The loose brick was now above him, but at least he could reach it.

The trouble was that he couldn't reach the rope. It dangled tantalisingly close, but his outstretched fingers could not quite brush it. Far overhead, he could see Rose Rita and Mrs

Jaeger looking down the shaft. He heard Rose Rita's echoing voice: "What happened?"

"I fell!" Lewis shouted. "I have to have more rope! Hurry!" They began to haul the rope up, and to keep from going completely insane, Lewis pried out the loose brick.

When he saw what was behind it, he knew he had truly solved the riddle.

Glowing with its own light was a jewel. It might have been a ruby, but a huge one—at least three inches across. It had been carved into the shape of a heart. Not a valentine heart, but a model of an actual human heart.

And it beat with its own evil inner life. The glow pulsed regularly, like a real heartbeat. Lewis quickly grabbed the jewel and forced it into his jeans pocket. He was panting for breath, feeling as if he were freezing.

Then he heard sounds from above. He looked up and could not believe what he was seeing.

Rose Rita was sliding down the rope towards him.

Lewis knew how terrified she must be.

And suddenly his own fear fell away.

Rose Rita hated closed-in spaces more than anything in the world. Yet she was sliding steadily towards Lewis. If Rose Rita could come to rescue him, he could try to save his uncle and his friends.

He just hoped it would not be too late.

Rose Rita reached the end of the rope. She had it tied around her left wrist, and she flailed out with her right hand. In a strangled, choking voice, she said, "Here! Grab hold!"

"You can't hold my weight!" said Lewis. "Let me give you what I found—"

"We're both going back up," Rose Rita declared. "Take my hand!"

Lewis grabbed her wrist. She groaned as he pulled himself up, bracing his feet on the slippery bricks. He got his other hand on the end of the rope, clung on for dear life, and said, "Go! I'm OK now! Go!"

Rose Rita began to climb. Lewis wound the free end of the rope around his left wrist and held on with both hands as Rose Rita's movement swung him this way and that. She paused halfway up, breathing hard and whimpering. "I can't!" she said.

Lewis climbed up below her. "You can do it. Come on! Race you to the top! It's just like climbing the rope in P.E. class!"

"I can't do that either!" wailed Rose Rita.

"Next year you'll be able to!" shouted Lewis. "Because we're practising! Put your bottom hand on top! Grip the rope with your knees! One inch at a time, if you have to!"

Slowly, Rose Rita began to climb again. Lewis thought his arms would pop out of their sockets. He followed Rose Rita up, inch by painful inch. At last Mrs Jaeger helped haul Rose Rita over the edge of the well, and then both of them leaned down to give Lewis a hand up. He emerged into twilight. The sun was down behind the trees. "T-t-time?" he asked.

"Well past eight o'clock," Mrs Jaeger said. "Oh, dear. We'd better hurry!"

From the direction of the ruined farmhouse,

someone laughed harshly. "Hurry off? But you have to stay! I insist!"

Rose Rita screamed in alarm, and Lewis felt as if he was going to pass out.

From the shadows near the old house a tall, white-haired figure stepped out. She was holding a magic wand.

Ermine Moote had found them.

CHAPTER FOURTEEN

For a moment no one said a word. Then Ermine Moote stepped a little closer. "Now, what were you doing down there, hmm? I wonder. Is there a secret passageway, perhaps? What have you meddled in?"

Lewis was thinking furiously. In one pocket he had the ruby heart. In the other, he had—well, something that might come in handy. "We know all about what was under the bridge," he said.

"I doubt that," said Ermine Moote. "I doubt it very much."

"It's the ashes of old Jebediah Clabbernong," said Rose Rita. "He was supposed to change into a Great Old One, but something went wrong with the spell, and he wound up as some kind of monster."

Lewis saw Ermine Moote's eyes grow round with surprise, then narrow with suspicion. "No one knew that! No one but my husband and I!"

Mrs Jaeger crossed her arms. "You would be surprised," she said in a calm voice. "The Capharnaum County Magicians Society knows much more than you suspect. And they are meeting tonight to deal with your precious red star and all the rest."

Lewis put his hand in his pocket. He found what was inside and gripped it tightly. "Did you know that your husband is going to leave you behind? He told me so. He said he was going to be the only one who changed, and all the other humans would be wiped off the face of the Earth. And that includes you!"

"The worm wouldn't dare!" shouted Mrs Moote. "Why, I was the witch who knew all about the Clabbernongs and their magic! I married Mephistopheles Moote to get close to Elihu Clabbernong! My husband was just a country lawyer then—but he was Elihu's attorney! Between us, we got Elihu to tell us many things. If only the old man had lived a few more months, we would have forced all his secrets from him, including—" She broke off, then laughed nastily. "Of course," she said. "Of course! You found what Elihu had hidden! So it was in the well, was it? Why, with that, I can restore Jebediah Clabbernong's memory and awareness! I won't even need Mephisto! Who has it? You, girl? Or you, Lewis Barnavelt?"

"You can't have it!" Lewis shouted, tightening his grip.

"Oh, but I can," replied Mrs Moote, leering. "I can turn you into a rat—or I can fry you right where you stand and take it from the ashes! It's in your pocket! Give it to me now, and maybe I'll go easy on you!"

"Don't do it, Lewis," said Rose Rita. "She's bluffing!"

Mrs Moote nicked her wand to the side. A jet of crimson light shot from it and struck the old farmhouse.

With a groan of wood and a clatter of tin, it collapsed, ending up a cloud of choking dust. Mrs Moote stalked forwards, her eyes blazing, the wand pointed at Lewis.

"Bluffing, am I?"

Lewis held out his fist. "Don't hurt me," he pleaded. " And don't hurt my friends. Let us go, and you can have this."

"No!" said Mrs Jaeger.

But she was too late. The triumphant Ermine Moote was reaching out for what Lewis held.

And he dropped it into her outstretched hand. For an instant, the rivet from the wizard's bridge lay on her bony palm. Then it flared to life, its colours shooting like spears. "No!" screamed Ermine Moote, dropping her wand. Frantically she shook her hand, but the rivet clung there as if it had been welded on. "No!" With a loud shriek, she ran stumbling past the ruin of the farmhouse, vanishing in the cloud of dust. Lewis ground his teeth at the gobbling, maddened yelps she made. "What did I do?" he asked. "I was just trying to buy time—"

"Hush, dear," said Mrs Jaeger. "I can guess where that piece of iron came from. You didn't know about its power. It isn't your fault—" Then something unexpected happened.

On the ground, the wand that Ermine Moote had brandished suddenly snapped in two, with a sharp noise like a gun shot.

Mrs Jaeger took a long, deep breath. "It's over for her," she said. "When a magician dies, his or her wand breaks. Let's go."

What was left of Mrs Moote lay on the rutted path to the road. It was a vaguely woman-shaped mass of ashy grey dust. One arm must have been outstretched. The rivet lay there, still gleaming with those unearthly colours.

"She—she dissolved," said Rose Rita.

"She was very old. Her whole body was held together by magic," explained Mrs Jaeger. "And that enchanted iron took away all her power. We may need it again. Lewis, you'd better pick it up. I *am* a witch, even if I'm not a very talented one. No telling what it might do to me."

Grimacing with distaste, Lewis plucked the rivet from the pile of ash and dust. With his sneakers squelching at every step, he ran with the others to Mrs Jaeger's car. They saw the Mootes' car nearby, off the far side of the road and half hidden in some rhododendrons. "We have to hurry," said Mrs Jaeger. "Midnight is coming, and now we have less than four hours."

Still, she drove very slowly. And she insisted on stopping at Lewis's house so he could change into dry jeans and shoes. "Dear, there's no sense in your coming down with pneumonia," she said firmly.

What with one thing and another, two hours passed before Mrs Jaeger pulled her car over on a hillside north of New Zebedee. By then the night sky was very dark, and when Lewis and Rose Rita climbed out of the car, Lewis didn't even have to glance up. The red comet was bright enough to give the whole countryside a faint tinge of scarlet.

The members of the Capharnaum County Magicians Society stood in a circle on the hilltop. Each of them held a lighted candle. Jonathan Barnavelt came hurrying over, his eyes wide with astonishment. "What in the world is going on?"

Lewis hastily tried to explain, with Rose Rita putting in a word now and then. Lewis pulled the ruby from his pocket and handed it to his uncle. "And there it is," he finished. "We think it holds Jebediah Clabbernong's soul."

"I think you're right," said Mrs Zimmermann, who had come over to listen. "Jonathan, we've been trying to raise a cone of protection for New Zebedee. From what Lewis tells us, it seems that Mephisto Moote has his sights set on the whole world. We have to change our plan."

"But we can't attack him with magic," objected Jonathan. "The spirit that Jebediah called from the depths or snared from space thrives on magic—feeds on it! Any magic we throw at it only makes it stronger—especially because Jebediah's ashes gave it a body."

Mrs Zimmermann touched her chin with one

finger. "Then maybe we throw our magic another way," she said thoughtfully.

At that moment, someone higher up on the hill shouted out, "Something is happening!"

Lewis and Rose Rita turned. Everyone was stumbling away from the summit of the hill. A few people had dropped their candles. Lewis blinked. A fog was forming up the slope. A swirling, glowing crimson fog. It pulsed almost like the throb of light in the ruby. Abruptly, it condensed—

"So," snarled Mephisto Moote. "All here in a pleasant little party, hey? And you didn't invite me!"

Mrs Zimmermann carried her umbrella. She raised it, and in an instant was transformed. Instead of her purple dress, she wore flowing black robes outlined in purple flame, and the umbrella had become a tall staff with a bright purple star at its tip. "Mephistopheles Moote," she said in a stern voice, "half your power is already gone! Your wife has tried to fight us and has failed!"

"Half my power?" sneered Moote. "My dear Mrs Florence Busybody Zimmermann, she was not a tenth of my power! Behold! I summon the Great Old One! No one can stand against him!" And he began to chant "Ry'leh! Ny'arleth! Yog-Shoggoth!" and other sounds that, to Lewis, meant nothing.

Again the crimson fog formed and condensed— and this time, from its depths, a terrible, shifting form stepped out. It was gigantic, twelve feet tall. Its writhing, boneless arms thrashed. It quivered and rippled, its face sliding all over its misshapen head. Around its feet, the grass immediately died, turning the crystalline grey of the vegetation at the Clabbernong farm. "Hunger!" it bawled in a terrible, thick voice. "I hunger!"

"That's Jebediah Clabbernong!" shouted Mrs Zimmermann. "Or what's left of him! Is that what *you* expect to be, Mephisto? A slobbering, lurching pile of mindless jelly?"

"I will be transfigured!" howled Moote. "I will live forever!" He lifted a trembling finger and pointed to Mrs Zimmermann. "Destroy her!" he shouted. "Destroy them all!"

Mrs Zimmermann lifted her wand and spread her other hand as if she were about to cast a spell. The monster halted and braced itself, obviously anticipating a blast of magic. Then, suddenly, Mrs Zimmermann turned and yelled, "Run for it, everyone! No magic!"

The crowd of people streamed down the hill. Jonathan hustled Mrs Zimmermann and the others into his car, and they roared away. Lewis turned in his seat and stared back. The monster was thrashing and bellowing. It struck a tree, and the tree shattered as if it were made of glass.

"Whoosh!" gasped Mrs Zimmermann. "Everyone all right?"

"Yes, Florence," Mrs Jaeger said. She was in the back seat with Lewis and Rose Rita. "I left my car!"

"We'll get it later," said Jonathan. "I'm sure we'll be the target Moote will follow. He wanted us to use our magic. Now he'll be angry. We have to do something—and before twelve o'clock! But what?"

"Uncle Jonathan," said Lewis, "I have the rivet from the old bridge."

"Good for you," replied Uncle Jonathan. "Well, Florence? Any ideas?"

"The spark of one, perhaps," said Mrs Zimmermann. "Let's get to the place where the old bridge used to stand. Time's a-wasting!"

Twice before they reached the spot, Lewis thought it was all over. Near town, the monstrous jelly creature popped up just ahead of them and swiped at the car. Jonathan yanked the steering wheel, and the car's right tyres jolted on to the grassy shoulder. The beast's squelchy tentacle left a long, slimy smear down the driver's-side windows. Then, just south of town, Mephisto Moote stood on a rise near the road, waving a wand. Fireballs shot from the wand, sending sizzling red globes that whizzed towards them. Two missed, but the third struck the car roof a glancing blow, with white-hot sparks of metal flying.

At last, with the roar of tyres on gravel, Jonathan pulled the Muggins Simoon off close to the new bridge. They all spilled out. Mrs Zimmermann said quickly, "Jonathan, you and I have to work out a spell. Everyone else, watch out for trouble! If Mr Moote and his horrible pet show up, you'll have to hold them off. We can't help you there. One way or another, we have to end this tonight."

"I'm scared," said Rose Rita.

Jonathan laughed, surprising Lewis. "Welcome to the club," he said. Then, to Mrs Zimmermann, he added, "OK, Pruny Face, I'm ready to help. What do we have to do?"

While the two of them put their heads together, Mrs Jaeger, Lewis, and Rose Rita kept watch. The road lay deserted. Overhead, the comet neared its zenith, its fiery tail streaming off to the east. Lewis had just begun to breathe easier when everything fell silent. The crickets and other night insects stopped their chirping, as though a knob had been turned.

"They're here," said Mrs Jaeger, waving the

wooden spoon she used as a wand. "I don't know where, but they're here."

Lewis switched on his torch. He shone it up and down the road, but nothing moved. Rose Rita muttered, "Maybe they're going to—"

And then Lewis heard a bellow coming from behind him! He spun. The terrible creature was climbing up the bank beyond Uncle Jonathan and Mrs Zimmermann. At its touch, all the grass wilted immediately. Right behind the monster, Mephisto Moote floated in the air, his face contorted in hatred. "Stop this foolishness!" he screamed, setting his feet on the ground again. "Pitiful worms, your death has come for you!"

'Lewis heard Mrs Zimmermann say, "All right, Jonathan?"

Uncle Jonathan said, "Lewis, shine that light on me, if you please."

The monster was fifteen feet away. It took a step forwards, its awful, mismatched eyes rolling. The choking stench of it made Lewis retch. But he turned the torch towards his uncle.

Jonathan held up the ruby. "See this, Moote? Know what it is? *You* know what it is, don't you—Jebediah?"

The creature stopped, shaking. It made a blubbing sound, almost like a question.

"There's some dim part inside you that knows what this is," continued Jonathan.

"Shut up, shut up!" screamed Moote. "You—you parlour magician! I'll destroy you!"

"Then you will also destroy the soul of Jebediah Clabbernong!" shouted Jonathan.

The creature quivered all over. "S-soulll?" it moaned in its awful, burbling voice. "Ss-ss-oullll?"

Shrieking in rage, Moote said, "If he won't take care of you, I will!" He raised his wand—and the monster whipped around, one of its lashing tentacles striking him hard in the chest. With a howl of pain and hatred, Moote stumbled backwards and fell off the creek bank. No splash followed.

Jonathan said, "Show our friend the rivet, Lewis."

Lewis held up the piece of iron. Its colours were unusually bright. The thing that had been Jebediah Clabbernong made a horrible gurgling snarl.

"That's right," said Jonathan. "It's what kept you safely underwater all those years. Now, what would happen if we put *this*"—Jonathan raised the ruby heart—"together with *that*? Especially with the Red Star overhead?"

The creature struck forwards, lashing with a tentacle. Jonathan flung the ruby heart up and yelled, "*Now*, Florence!"

With her robes billowing, Mrs Zimmermann spoke a spell and pointed the crystal on her wand towards the heart. It zoomed into the air—and Lewis felt the rivet jerk from his grasp! Two glowing streaks shot high into the darkness.

With a scream of terror, the monster reached up, up—and then it *streamed* away, turning to a silvery liquid, pouring into the night sky, trying to reach the streaking heart!

For a few moments they all watched. The three gleams of light went higher, higher—until they gradually dimmed and vanished. "Will they ever come down?" asked Rose Rita.

"They will come down, if that's what you call it, on the surface of the comet," said Mrs Zimmermann. For the first time Lewis noticed that her robes were gone, and her wand. She clutched her simple black umbrella again. Only the crystal knob shone with a purple star at its heart.

Jonathan had walked over to the stream and was shining the torch down. "Yuck," he said.

Lewis joined him. What was left of Mephisto Moote was a drift of grey powder on the surface of the creek. "What happened?" he asked.

"That thing touched him," said Uncle Jonathan. "It sucked the life force right out of him. Left him just a brittle husk. When he fell, he crumbled."

"Is it over?" asked Rose Rita.

Mrs Zimmermann sighed. "Only time will tell."

Then the night insects began to sing again.
Lewis thought he had never heard a more
comforting sound.

CHAPTER FIFTEEN

The summer passed. September came, and school began again. The whole time, Lewis felt jumpy, as if something had not quite ended. He found it hard to sleep, because terrifying dreams kept jolting him awake. Rose Rita confessed that she too was having nightmares. The thought of the strange creature and the red comet still troubled her.

Then, one calm Friday evening, Mrs Zimmermann came over to make dinner for Jonathan, Lewis, and Rose Rita. Lewis and

Rose Rita were in the kitchen helping her whip potatoes when they all heard Jonathan shout, "Quick! Come in here!"

They hurried to the parlour. Jonathan pointed to the TV screen. "Listen to this!"

The news announcer was saying, "Astronomers now believe that the unusual red comet visible last July must have been destroyed. It vanished behind the sun in August and should have reappeared by the first of this month. Something, scientists say, probably collided with it, perhaps a small asteroid. That was enough to knock the comet off its normal orbit, and it either broke up completely because of the sun's gravity or, more likely, fell straight into the sun. In other news . . ."

"Well!" said Mrs Zimmermann. "Good news if I ever heard it. That's one less thing to worry about!"

"It wasn't an asteroid that hit it," said Rose Rita, her voice filled with understanding. "It was a ruby and a rivet and a gloppy mess."

"It sure was," agreed Jonathan. "All of it

jet-propelled by Frizzy Wig's dandy magic spell, designed to send everything up to the red comet that was supposed to be holding the Great Old Ones inside it. That was a stroke of genius, Florence, directing the magic at those things instead of at Moote and his monster."

"Thank you, Brush Mush," replied Mrs Zimmermann with a smile. "Though I really didn't know whether it would work or not! I'm glad that my aim was accurate."

"Well, *I'm* glad the Mootes have departed this vale of tears for good and all," said Jonathan. "Those rats had planned all this for years. Why, I found out that they were the two citizens who complained about the old bridge over Wilder Creek in the first place. They were the ones who persuaded the county to tear it down—because they knew the red comet was coming, and they wanted that creature to be free when it got here."

"Was it really Jebediah Clabbernong?" asked Rose Rita.

Mrs Zimmermann replied, "It was—in part.

And the other part was a creature from some other dimension that rode to Earth on a meteorite. I think it started out as a shapeless blob of jelly. After Elihu poured old Jebediah's ashes into the creek, the blob soaked them up. It was just human enough to want a soul and monstrous enough to draw the life out of anything it could touch."

Uncle Jonathan stroked his red beard. "So good riddance to Mephistopheles and Ermine Moote, who set the dreadful thing free. Florence, I told you the first time I saw those two birds that they'd get themselves mixed up in some diabolical plot—"

"The Mootes!" Lewis yelled. "You were talking about the Mootes! My gosh, Uncle Jonathan, I overheard you say that. I thought you were talking about Rose Rita and me!"

Jonathan looked astonished. Then he threw back his head and laughed. "Lewis, you should know me better by now!" he said. "Mind you, I'm not really happy about your sneaking around and climbing down wells—but Lewis, you're more than just my nephew. You're my whole family. My whole world!"

"And everyone else's whole world is safe now, right?" asked Rose Rita, sounding anxious.

Mrs Zimmermann put a hand on her shoulder. "It's safe forever from the mad Mootes and from old Jebediah Clabbernong's restless spirit," she assured her young friend. Lewis saw Rose Rita finally relax. Mrs Zimmermann patted her shoulder and added, "And if anything else awful comes along, I'd say the four of us have some powerful magic to pit against it."

"We've got friendship," agreed Jonathan. "And people who look out for each other, and people who act for the best even when they're shaking in their boots from terror. And we also have some halfway decent food, or my nose deceives me!"

They had a scrumptious dinner. Then, later, in the cool, clear air of early fall, they went into the back yard and spent an hour gazing through the telescope at the stars and planets. None of them looked the least bit frightening.

They were all wonderful, bright, beautiful, and mysterious.

Lewis felt the worries and fears of the summer falling away from him as he lost himself in staring through the eyepiece. Around him, the universe wheeled on, orderly and regular, and a million brilliant and kindly lights eased the darkness and made the face of the night less lonely. After a long while, everyone went inside again, and that night Lewis slept deeply and peacefully, and his dreams were happy ones.

The End

John Bellairs (1938–1991) was an award-winning American author of many gothic mystery novels for children and young adults, including *The House With a Clock in Its Walls*, which received both the New York Times Outstanding Book of the Year Award and the American Library Association Children's Books of International Interest Award, *The Lamp from the Warlock's Tomb*, which won the Edgar Award and *The Spectre from the Magician's Museum*, which won the New York Public Library 'Best Books for Teen Age' Award.

Brad Strickland has written more than eighty-five published books, including entries in the Lewis Barnavelt and Johnny Dixon series, following the death of the original series creator, John Bellairs. He is a Professor Emeritus of English and lives in Georgia with his wife, Barbara.

Have you read the previous book?

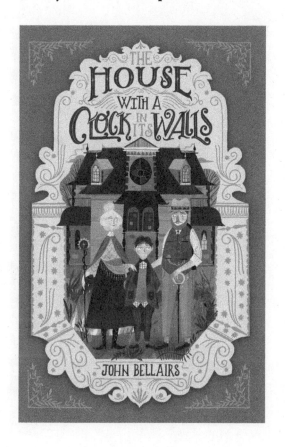

Piccadilly
PRESS

Have you read the previous book?

Piccadilly
PRESS

Have you read the previous book?

Piccadilly
PRESS

Have you read the previous book?

Have you read the previous book?

Piccadilly
PRESS

Have you read the previous book?

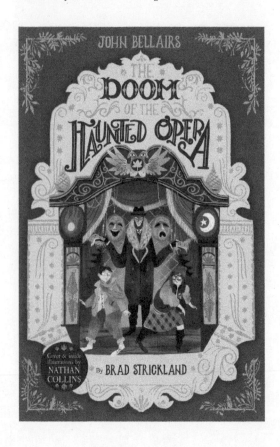

Piccadilly
PRESS

Have you read the previous book?

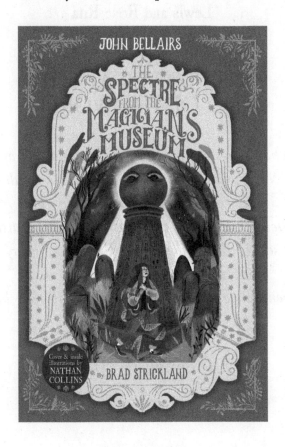

Piccadilly
PRESS

Thank you for choosing a Piccadilly Press book.

If you would like to know more about our authors, our books or if you'd just like to know what we're up to, you can find us online.

www.piccadillypress.co.uk

And you can also find us on:

We hope to see you soon!